"What's going on, Lily?"

Lily closed her eyes and braced herself against the tone in Eric's voice. She couldn't allow him to change her mind.

"Nothing's going on. All I want is a baby."

"By artificial insemination? Lily, you're twenty-eight years old. You've got plenty of time to have a baby. Besides, what's wrong with the old-fashioned way? Meet a guy, get married, create a baby...."

"Marriage isn't for me," she said firmly. "I've already tried it, remember?"

Eric reached for her hand, warming her with gentle reassurance. "You're still sad about losing David, Lily. But someday you'll feel differently. You'll want to get married again."

"No, I won't. I just can't," she sadly insisted. "The women in my family are jinxed when it comes to marriage. Didn't I ever tell you?"

Jinxed? What in the world was she talking about?

Dear Reader,

Babies—who can resist them? Celebrating the wonder of new life—and new love—Silhouette Romance introduces a brand-new series, BUNDLES OF JOY. In these wonderful stories, couples are brought together by babies—and kept together by love! We hope you enjoy all six BUNDLES OF JOY books in April. Look for more in the months to come.

Favorite author Suzanne Carey launches the series with *The Daddy Project*. Sherry Tompkins is caring for her infant nephew and she needs help from the child's father, Mike Ruiz. Is marrying Mike the best way to find out if he's daddy material?

Lindsay Longford brings us *The Cowboy, the Baby and the Runaway Bride*. T. J. Tyler may have been left at the altar years ago by Callie Jo Murphy, but now this rugged cowboy and his adorable baby boy are determined to win her back.

Lullaby and Goodnight is a dramatic new story from Sandra Steffen about a single mom on the run. LeAnna Chadwick longs to stay in the shelter of Vince Macelli's arms, but the only way to protect her child is to leave the man she loves.

The excitement continues with *Adam's Vow*, Karen Rose Smith's book about one man's search for his missing daughters—and the beautiful, mysterious woman who helps him. Love and laughter abound in Pat Montana's *Babies Inc.*, a tale of two people who go into the baby business together and find romance in the process. And debut author Christine Scott brings us the heartwarming *Hazardous Husband*.

I hope you will enjoy BUNDLES OF JOY. Until next month—

Happy Reading!

Anne Canadeo
Senior Editor
Silhouette Romance

Please address questions and book requests to:
Silhouette Reader Service
U.S.: 3010 Walden Ave., P.O. Box 1325, Buffalo, NY 14269
Canadian: P.O. Box 609, Fort Erie, Ont. L2A 5X3

HAZARDOUS HUSBAND

Christine Scott

Silhouette
ROMANCE™
Published by Silhouette Books
America's Publisher of Contemporary Romance

To Kristy, my little redhead with a mind of her own.
May your life be filled with love and happiness always.

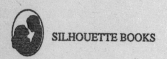

SILHOUETTE BOOKS

ISBN 0-373-19077-8

HAZARDOUS HUSBAND

Copyright © 1995 by Susan Rundé

This edition published by arrangement with Harlequin Enterprises B.V.

® and TM are trademarks of Harlequin Enterprises B.V., used under
license. Trademarks indicated with ® are registered in the United States
Patent and Trademark Office, the Canadian Trade Marks Office and in
other countries.

Printed in U.S.A.

CHRISTINE SCOTT

grew up in Illinois but currently lives in St. Louis, Missouri. A former teacher, she now writes full time. When she isn't writing romances, she spends her time caring for her husband and three children. In between car pools, baseball games and dance lessons, Christine always finds time to pick up a good book and read about...love.

There are only two lasting bequests we can hope to give our children. One of these is roots; the other, wings.

—Hodding Carter

Dear Readers,

Babies are irresistible. Whether it be their chubby cheeks or their breath-stealing smiles, something about babies can make even the most resolute woman perk up and listen to the ticking of her biological clock. I speak from experience, having been thrice bitten by the baby lust.

But, alas, even babies grow up. Kevin, my oldest, is now a teenager. Kristy, my own little redhead, is eleven. And Scotty, doomed always to be called the baby of the family, is eight. Now I've traded three o'clock feedings, diaper changes and teething for baseball practices, car pools and braces.

I can imagine most women will be able to relate to Lily's wish to have a baby. After all, one look into a pair of baby blues—*real* baby blues, that is—can have even the best of us sighing with a maternal desire. I hope you enjoy reading about Lily and Eric's hazardous road to romance as much as I've enjoyed writing it.

Just be careful…the baby lust is contagious.

Christine Scott

tary. "Hold all calls." He hung up the phone and turned to Lily. "We need to talk."

Lily closed her eyes and braced herself against the soothing tone of Eric's voice. She reminded herself there was a reason Eric was a successful divorce attorney and the majority of his clients were female. He had a gift—the power of persuasion. Or, as her grandmother would say, he could charm the pants off any woman. She couldn't allow him to change her mind. She wanted this baby.

"What's going on, Lily?"

Eric's voice sounded close. Her eyes flew open. He'd moved. He now sat in the companion chair at her side. She felt small next to him. Small, but not easily intimidated. "Nothing's going on. All I want is a baby."

"By artificial insemination."

She stared down at her hands, balled in her lap. "Yes, by artificial insemination."

"Lily, you're only twenty-eight years old. You've got plenty of time to have a baby. Besides, what's wrong with the old-fashioned way? Meet a guy, get married, create a baby. Marriage isn't something I'd recommend for everyone, but for you—"

Marriage? A dull pain thumped in her chest as the word conjured up hurtful memories. She'd met Eric the same time as she'd met David, at a retirement party for one of their co-workers. She was supposed to deliver a cake and leave, but David and Eric convinced her to stay for the party.

Eric's good looks and charm had caught her eye, but it was David's stability that won her heart. Instinctively she knew that with Eric a woman could expect a roller-coaster relationship—a thrill a minute, but over in the blink of an eye. David, on the other hand, was a man she could rely on. To him, she wasn't just the flavor of the month; she was the main course in a meal he would never tire of. Her relationship with David had represented the very thing missing in her life—a sense of permanence.

Despite the fact that they were opposites, David and Eric had been lifetime friends, classmates and then business colleagues. David had had the utmost respect for Eric. When she and David had married, Eric had been the best man.

"Marriage isn't for me, either," she said firmly. "I've already tried it, remember?"

Eric tossed the donor release form onto his desk. He reached for her hand, squeezing it, warming her with gentle reassurance. "David died, Lily. His death had nothing to do with your marriage."

"Our marriage had *everything* to do with David's death." She snatched her hand away. "I killed him, Eric. I killed David."

Eric felt as though the air had been knocked out of him and Lily had dealt the blow. He stared at her for a full minute, unsure what to say.

When David had died, Lily had withdrawn into a protective shell, pushing away Eric and everyone who cared about her. But in the past year or so, Eric had caught a glimmer of the old Lily, the spitfire of life whom he'd grown fond of. Now he couldn't help but wonder if all the progress she'd made had been just a facade, if she were still protecting herself from the pain of David's death.

"Lily, David died in a plane crash," he said, choosing his words carefully. "You were hundreds of miles away. There's no way you could have killed him."

Stark green eyes riveted him. "As surely as if I'd had a gun and shot him, I killed him. I should never have married David. My mother, my grandmother—they both

warned me. They told me what would happen if I did."
She shook her head. "But I thought it was just the ima-
ginings of eccentric women. I should have known it was
the truth."

"Lily, you aren't making sense." A hint of exaspera-
tion touched his voice. "What was the truth?"

She blinked. "The curse, of course."

She was in worse shape than he'd thought. Lily was to-
tally unhinged. "Curse?"

"I'm not crazy, Eric," she said, laughing as though
she'd read his mind.

He felt his face warm with embarrassment. "I didn't
say you were."

"No, but you were thinking it." A smile lingered.
"Don't worry, Eric. It's taken me years to finally accept
the curse."

Frustrated, he fell back into his chair. He placed an elbow on the armrest, leaned his chin on an upturned palm
and studied her. Petite. Though they were just friends, he
wasn't blind to the eye-pleasing way her sky-blue sun-
dress hugged the curves of her body. Dark, auburn hair
curled about her shoulders. A flawless, creamy-white
complexion. Dimples that danced in her cheeks when she
smiled. Yep, she was the same woman who'd walked into
his office unexpectedly half an hour ago and asked to talk
to him about an urgent matter. Eric just couldn't shake
the feeling that he was seeing her for the first time.

When David died, Eric had made it a point to visit Lily
at least once a week. At first these visits had been a matter of obligation, an obligation he'd felt to his best
friend's widow. But after three years he continued the
visits because of the friendship that had evolved between
them.

He felt closer to Lily than any woman he'd ever known. Which was why he was shocked. He'd had no warning. No inkling that Lily was still so deeply troubled by David's death.

He took a deep breath. "I'm probably going to regret asking this, but what exactly is this curse?"

Lily folded her hands in her lap and straightened her shoulders. Eric fought the urge to smile. She looked as though she were a student preparing for a recitation.

"You've met my family."

"A couple of times. At the wedding." He swallowed hard. "And the funeral."

"Didn't you notice anything different about them?"

He tried to picture Lily's family in his mind. Let's see, there was her grandmother, a nice blue-haired lady with an age-wizened face. Her mother, who had reddish hair like Lily and was pretty for her age. He couldn't honestly say he knew either woman well. Before he'd met Lily, her mother had retired from teaching at ASU and had moved to Sedona, taking Lily's grandmother with her. She was an artist, a sculptor, he believed—which wasn't exactly a conventional career, but not unusual. Eric frowned. Lily's family seemed like most others, concerned for one of their own.

"They seemed nice enough," he said. "They seemed . . . normal."

"Eric, there are no *men* in my family."

"No men?" He almost smiled again. "What are you trying to tell me, Lily? You were all conceived by artificial means?"

"No, we were not." She drew herself up tall, a picture of indignation. "We were all conceived in the natural way. Listen carefully, Eric. My grandfather died four months before my mother was born. A farming accident. Nana never remarried. My father crossed the street and was hit by a bus three days before I was born. My mother never remarried." Lily raised an eyebrow. "See a trend here?"

He rose to his feet. After he'd walked to the wall of windows overlooking downtown Phoenix, Eric stared at the mirage of buildings shimmering in the desert sun. He pressed a palm to the sun-warmed glass and tried to make sense of Lily's story.

Lily wanted a child. Whether he agreed to be the father was beside the point. The problem, as he saw it, was that Lily had never gotten over David's death.

He understood how hard it was to lose someone you loved. His own father had died when Eric was ten years old. Though the pain had faded, not a day went by that he didn't miss his dad. The tips of his fingers slid across the smooth glass as he fisted his hand.

Yes, he could understand Lily's suffering. But he also knew the time had come for her to put the suffering aside and get on with her life.

He turned to Lily. "What happened to David and your father and even your grandfather is just a coincidence."

Now it was her turn to give him a disbelieving look. "Every man who's married into my family has dropped dead within the first year of marriage. You call that a coincidence?"

He threw his hands up. "Okay, bad luck."

"Bad luck, humph." She crossed her arms. "Face it, Eric. The women in my family are black widows. Whether it's intentional or not, we kill off our mates. I don't want to marry and bury another husband just to have a baby."

"You're being ridiculous."

Her eyes narrowed. One pump-clad foot tapped a warning beat on the floor.

He'd roused Lily's famous temper. But it was too late to turn back. He had to make her see reason. "You're blaming yourself for David's death because you're afraid to get on with your life."

Lily stiffened. "Let's talk about blame, Eric. How about the business trip David took to Los Angeles? The one he took for you, Eric? The one that crashed? You were supposed to be on that plane."

A weight of pain pressed against his chest. He drew in a shaky breath. "Are you blaming me for David's death?"

She shook her head. "No, of course not. But you blame yourself. Don't you think I know the real reason you've been such a good friend to me these past few years? Guilt has a nasty way of making us see to our obligations."

A thick silence filled the air between them. The steady buzz of his intercom broke the tension. Eric strode to the desk, glad for the interruption. He picked up the phone. "Yes, Mrs. Hunter."

"You're due in court in twenty minutes, Eric," Mrs. Hunter said.

He flicked the sleeve of his shirt and glanced at his gold watch. "Right, I'll be leaving shortly."

He heard the whisper of silk as Lily uncrossed her legs and stood. Slowly he returned the phone to its cradle and faced her.

Her expression grim, she met his gaze. "If you agree to be a sperm donor, there'll be no obligations, financially or personally. I'm giving you a chance to clean the slate. I wouldn't be asking you to do this for me if it wasn't important. Will you at least think it over?"

"Of course I will. Lily, I don't want you to think—"

"Look, we've said enough for one day. You're busy, and I need to get back to the bakery. Call me when you've made a decision." With a swing of her auburn hair, Lily left his office.

Eric sank into the leather chair behind his desk and reached for the donor release form. No obligations. Bull. This agreement reeked with obligations. Of all the men in Phoenix, why did Lily have to ask him?

As far as he could see, this was a no-win situation. Damned if he did, damned if he didn't. If this were a case, he'd cut his losses and try to settle out of court. Except the stakes in this case were too high. His friendship with Lily was on the line.

"As far as decadent pleasures go, I think this one rates right up there at the top," Lily said, sighing.

A murmur of agreement sounded in Lily's bakery, The Finishing Touch.

"Don't rush. There's plenty of time," she said. "I want you to enjoy it."

Lily plunged her fork into another bite of her famous Sinfully Delicious Devil's Food Cake. The two women sitting across from her did the same. They were seated at a table in the corner of the bakery, which she had dubbed the Wedding Alcove.

A round archway separated the tiny alcove from the rest of the bakery. Decorated with white wicker furnishings, pink-and-green floral cushions and a background of lush, green plants, it was a place where her clients could shop for their wedding cakes in relative privacy.

Lily felt a familiar rush of pride as she glanced around the place. She loved to create beautiful things. When she was a child, her mother—a talented artist in her own right—put a crayon in Lily's hand, gave her a sheet of paper and allowed her to indulge her creative urges. It hadn't taken long for either of them to realize she'd inherited her mother's talent.

Rather than follow in her mother's footsteps, she'd forged her own artistic path. After graduating from college with a degree in fine arts, Lily took a job as an apprentice decorator at a local bakery. Instead of pen and paper as her tools for design, she used cakes and icing. Each cake she created was unique, as much a work of art as any painting or sculpture.

David's death had prompted her to open her own bakery. She'd hoped the demands of running a business would keep her too busy to dwell on her loss. For the most part, this had proved true. But the bakery provided much more than an escape from grief. It involved her in two things missing in her life—love and marriage.

She would be lying if she said she didn't long for the chance to love again, to share her life with one special man. However, she'd accepted the fact that she could never marry again. Regret rippled through her, tightening her chest with its familiar pain. She knew in her heart she wasn't strong enough to risk falling in love, only to lose another husband as she'd lost David.

"Mrs. Gerard, this is the best chocolate cake I've ever eaten." The thin young woman with blond hair cooed her appreciation, pulling Lily out of her reverie. "Momma, I just have to have it for the groom's cake."

Momma swallowed a mouthful of cake and threw a skeptical glance in her daughter's direction. "But, baby, it's chocolate. You can't have chocolate icing on a wedding cake."

"Trust me, this cake tastes just as good with white icing as it does with chocolate," Lily said.

Momma's eyes narrowed. "Can you match it to the bridesmaids' dresses? They're lavender-and-white striped."

"No problem." With a confident smile, Lily reached for the book that pictured samples of her wedding cakes. The Finishing Touch logo was inscribed on the front cover. She flicked through the pages. "Here, this is a cake I did last spring. I call it Lavender and Lace."

Both women studied the photo. At the sound of their oohs of appreciation, Lily felt her muscles relax. Another sale, she told herself, trying to muster a token sense of accomplishment at the feat. Her efforts fell flat. No matter what she did, an unease seemed to have hung over her head ever since leaving Eric's office this morning.

Her mouth felt dry at the thought of Eric. Lily returned her plate of chocolate cake to the table and picked up her glass of ice water. She'd been on edge the entire day, wondering what Eric might do, wondering what she might do if Eric turned her down.

She could go back to the fertility clinic and browse through the catalog of nameless donors. The thought left her cold inside. Height, weight, hair color... the whole process felt as personal as shopping for next fall's wardrobe. Not what she had in mind when selecting a potential father for her baby.

She could give up. Maybe a baby just wasn't in her future. She considered what her life would be without a baby. The lonely nights, the empty house. No one to love. No one to share her life. A long shiver racked her body.

"Are you okay, Mrs. Gerard?"

Momma was watching her, concern in her eyes.

Lily put her glass on the table. "I'm fine. I just caught a chill."

"A chill? It's a 105 out there today." Momma motioned to the window overlooking the tiled courtyard.

Lily followed the direction of the woman's hand, then wished she hadn't. Across the courtyard, just beyond the Spanish-style water fountain, Eric was bearing down on the bakery.

Sans tie, his white shirt sleeves rolled up a couple of notches, mirrored sunglasses covering his eyes, he looked relaxed and dangerous. His loose-hipped swagger caught the attention of more than one passing female shopper as he crossed the courtyard of shops.

Lily felt an unexpected surge of irritation. How dared he be so relaxed, when she'd been on pins and needles all day long? He passed by the Wedding Alcove's window on his way to the bakery's front door. A tinkle of a bell heralded his arrival.

Eric's slow glance around the room came to rest on her. He lowered the sunglasses. Despite his sober expression, his brown eyes sparkled, revealing a familiar hint of amusement. Lily froze, unable to move from her chair. Yet she couldn't drag her eyes away from him, either.

With a grin, Eric gave her a mock salute. Before she could say a word, he disappeared behind the counter and into the kitchen. The sound of giggling females followed his exit.

Lily closed her eyes and counted to ten. This wasn't the first time Eric had visited her bakery. And it wasn't the first time he'd charmed her staff. But it *was* the first time his flirting bothered her.

Fifteen minutes later, she ushered Momma and the young bride-to-be out the door and placed the Closed sign in the front window. Late-day shadows stretched across the courtyard outside the bakery. As though on cue, the

kitchen staff sauntered into the showroom, ready to de-
part for the day.

"'Night, Lily."

Ann, her assistant baker, gave her arm a friendly
squeeze. Ann's usual reluctance to leave Lily alone in the
bakery was absent this evening.

She nodded toward the kitchen. "Eric's waiting for
you."

"I know." Lily forced a smile. "See you tomorrow."

The doorbell chimed Ann's exit. Lily's heart pounded
in her chest. She and Eric were alone.

Slowly she crossed the showroom and entered the
kitchen. The staff had cleaned and polished the room
from top to bottom. The stainless-steel counters gleamed.
The tile floor sparkled. Perched on a chair in the middle
of all this cleanliness was Eric, munching on a thick slice
of devil's food cake.

He waved his fork at her. "Lily, you make the best
chocolate cake in Phoenix."

"You're going to spoil your dinner," she scolded him,
ignoring the compliment.

"Okay, Mom," he said, grinning.

Her heart did a flip-flop at his choice of words. He
must have noticed a change in her expression. He sobered, his grin fading. Without another word, he reached
into his shirt pocket and drew out a sheet of paper. He
placed it on the counter and scooted it toward her.

Lily pulled up a stool to the counter and sat down
across from Eric. Her hand shook as she reached for the
donor consent form. Her gaze flew down the length of the
paper. There in a bold flourish was Eric's signature.

She gulped in a deep breath of air and pressed the form
to her chest. She glanced across the counter. Eric was
watching her.

"Thank you, Eric," she said, her voice barely a whisper.

He nodded, stabbing the cake with his fork. "It's been witnessed and notarized."

Startled, she glanced at the form. Mrs. Hunter's signature was neatly penned below Eric's. "You told your secretary? What did she say?"

"Nothing I do surprises Mrs. Hunter." His devilish grin returned. "Don't worry, Lily. She's the soul of discretion."

A strained silence filled the room.

Eric was the first to break it. "So, now what do we do?"

"You'll need to have a blood test to make sure that our blood types are compatible. I'll call the clinic first thing tomorrow morning. Then we wait. I've been taking my temperature and charting my cycle for the past few months. You probably won't have to—" she cleared her throat "—to donate for another couple of weeks. I'll give you a call when it's time."

Eric shoved the remainder of his cake around on his plate, no longer seeming interested in eating.

Lily pushed herself to her feet and strode to her office. She returned, gripping a pamphlet in her hand. "The doctor gave me this to read. You may want to read it, too, so you have an idea what to expect."

Reluctantly, Eric took the pamphlet.

She pointed to the back page. "You can start practicing a few of these things as soon as possible."

"No smoking. No alcohol. No hot tubs." He glanced at her. "No briefs?"

She shrugged. "Boxers are better for your circulation. If you don't have any, there's a men's store just across the courtyard. I could—"

"That's quite all right, Lily. I can buy my own boxers." He continued reading. "Abstinence?" His voice boomed. "I feel as though I've signed up for two weeks at a monastery."

"Eric, these are just suggestions, ways to stoke up your sperm count." A small vein at his temple pulsed a vigorous beat. Her nervousness grew. He couldn't change his mind. Not now. "The higher your sperm count, the fewer times you'll have to... to donate."

"Times?" The single word echoed against the walls of the empty kitchen.

She smiled weakly. "Those little tadpoles don't always hit the mark on the first try, you know."

"How many times?"

She shrugged. "Two, maybe three times tops. Are you still going to help me?"

"I said I would, didn't I?"

Slouched in his seat, staring down at the pamphlet, he appeared anything but thrilled at the prospect.

"Eric, why did you agree to do this for me?" She winced as her voice trembled.

Still staring down at the pamphlet, he remained quiet for a long moment. "Not out of guilt," he said finally. He looked up, his brown eyes penetrating. "I want you to know something, Lily. Our friendship may have started out of obligation, but that's not what's kept it going three years. I care about you."

"I care about you, too." She felt the nagging burden of doubt being lifted from her shoulders. Now more than ever she needed the reassurance of Eric's friendship. "So, why are you helping me?"

"I may not agree with your decision. I may not even *want* to help you." He slammed the pamphlet down on the counter. "But if it's important to you, I have to help."

She glanced away, trying to swallow the lump of guilt that had formed in her throat. She should do the honorable thing and let him off the hook. But having a baby was too important for her.

"Now it's my turn," he said.

She glanced at him in surprise.

"Why did you ask *me* to be a sperm donor?" he inquired, his expression serious.

His question caught her off-guard. When she'd decided on artificial insemination, Eric had been her one and only choice. She knew he was kind, healthy and intelligent. She didn't know much about his family background. Lily stole an appreciative glance at the sculptured lines of his face. Obviously he came from a good gene pool.

She bit her lower lip. Drop-dead good looks notwithstanding, the most important reason she had chosen Eric to father her child was that he was her best friend. And in all the years they'd been friends, he'd shown no romantic interest in her. She felt safe asking him to be a sperm donor. Eric was in no danger of being next on her list of dead lovers.

"At first I considered an anonymous donor," she said, breaking the silence. "But that seemed so impersonal. And asking someone I knew seemed risky. What if he got the wrong idea and tried to pressure me into a relationship? I can't risk falling in love and marrying again. I won't cause another man's death."

Eric released a terse breath of air. "Lily, I want to make this perfectly clear. I don't believe for a minute that you had anything to do with David's death."

"It doesn't matter whether you believe it, Eric. I do. Which is why you're going to make the perfect sperm donor."

His gaze was wary. "Oh? Why is that?"

"Because we're friends, Eric. Just friends, nothing more. If there was any sort of physical attraction between us, surely it would have surfaced by now."

Eric said nothing. He shifted in his chair.

Lily continued, "Besides, I know about your aversion to marriage. Not that I agree with you. I think, if you really wanted to, you'd make some woman a wonderful husband."

"Here we go again."

"I can't help it if I believe in the sanctity of marriage. For everyone but me, that is. What's wrong with settling down with one special woman?"

"For one thing, we live in a community-property state."

"This is the nineties, Eric. Not every woman is after your money."

He humphed his disbelief.

She glared at him. "You really are a cynic, aren't you?"

"I've worked hard for what I have, Lily. If you'd helped end as many marriages as I have, you'd have doubts, also."

"Being a divorce lawyer has warped you."

"Owning a bakery specializing in wedding cakes has left you with a lopsided view of marriage. Believe me, most couples may start out their marriages with romantic dreams of a happy future, but chances are they'll end up in divorce court, slugging it out to the bitter end."

They'd been through this conversation before. Lily had given up trying to convince Eric that bachelorhood was a lonely state. They simply didn't see marriage in the same light. To her, marriage was a beautiful, unattainable dream. She would do anything to be guaranteed a lifetime of happiness with the man she loved. Eric, on the other hand, broke out in a cold sweat at the thought of making a commitment, whether financial or emotional.

She sighed. "At least I was right. You're going to be the perfect sperm donor."

He raised a brow in silent question.

"As a friend, you're wonderful. But as a prospective husband, you're terrible. Face it, Eric. The desert would have to freeze over before I'd marry someone as cynical as you."

Chapter Two

Lily Gerard had some nerve.

Ten days later, Eric found himself still stewing over Lily's parting words. *Face it, Eric. The desert would have to freeze over before I'd marry someone as cynical as you.* He ground his teeth, recalling the way she'd laughed, rubbing salt into an already wounded pride. What's so funny about telling him he was the last man on earth she'd consider marrying?

Why was he letting it bother him?

With her family's track record of killing off husbands, he should be glad he wasn't on Lily's list of possible marriage candidates.

But still, after he had agreed to do her a favor—correction, a huge favor—she'd had the nerve to insult him. Agreeing to be a sperm donor should rate some sort of respect, shouldn't it?

And what about this no-physical-attraction nonsense? Eric scowled. Lots of women found him appealing. Tons of them, in fact. Wasn't he good enough for Lily?

He'd always considered Lily an exceptionally beautiful woman. He'd have to be a complete idiot not to be tempted by her physical attributes. Not that he'd ever acted on that attraction. The time never seemed right. First there had been David's death. Lily had needed comfort, not someone trying to get her into his bed. Then their friendship got in the way.

Eric had dated plenty of women. But he'd never had a female friend before. He felt comfortable with Lily. He could take her out for dinner and the theater without worrying how the night would end. He could relax and talk to her about things he wouldn't dream of discussing with another woman. If their relationship took a turn and became intimate, all this would end. Sex had a way of changing a relationship. He didn't want to lose his friend.

His frown deepened. If sex changed a relationship, he couldn't help but wonder what having a baby would do to it.

He released an impatient breath. Despite his reservations, he'd gone to the fertility clinic and gotten his blood test. He'd even waited at the clinic long enough to find out they were a perfect match. Did he hear any of this from Lily? Hell, no. It had been well over a week since she'd called. If she wanted to talk to him, fine. But she was going to have to be the one to call and apologize first.

A niggling of doubt worked its way into his conscience, cooling his temper. He wasn't quite sure why he expected Lily to apologize. She'd spoken nothing but the truth. Over the years, he had acquired a cynical attitude toward love and marriage. But dammit, he had a right to be disillusioned.

He'd been engaged once, something he would never admit to Lily. It would give her too much hope for reforming his supposedly wretched bachelor existence. The engagement had been brief, lasting all of five months. Just out of law school, with a new job and a nagging college debt to repay, he still had had time to fall in love, or so he thought.

His ex-fiancée had been born to wealthy parents. Since he himself had come from a financially strapped background, her aristocratic breeding had been the one thing that had attracted him. It also proved to be their relationship's undoing. She didn't understand his need to work long hours in order to make his career a success. During their short engagement, they'd argued constantly over money, or rather the lack of it, and her feelings of neglect.

Gradually, her complaints had lessened. What he didn't realize was that she'd found someone else to ease her loneliness. Eric could still recall the shock he'd felt when she'd told him their engagement was off. That she was going to marry a retired businessman who had nothing but time and money to spend on her.

He drew in a slow breath, fighting the bitterness that threatened. He hadn't loved her, he realized now. After all these years, her betraying him with another man didn't bother him nearly as much as her using his lack of money as an excuse for leaving.

Eric pushed the painful memories from his mind. He'd wasted enough time brooding over the fickleness of love and marriage. He had work that demanded his full attention. He picked up a file from his desk, then slammed it back down. "I've got to be at a deposition in fifty minutes. Where's that accounting report?"

Mrs. Hunter reached across the desk and picked up a file. "Right where I left it for you last night. What's the matter with you, Eric? These past few days you've been in a real snit."

Scowling, Eric took the report. "I haven't been that bad, have I?"

"The worst I've ever seen you. Something's got your shorts in a wad. What's up?"

"Shorts?" His voice thundered. "What makes you think I'm wearing shorts?"

Mrs. Hunter gave an exasperated sigh. "It's just an expression, Eric."

A shrill ring interrupted them. Looking relieved at having a reason to end their conversation, Mrs. Hunter reached for the phone. "Eric Mitchell's office." Her face softened into a smile. "Hello, Lily."

Eric rolled his eyes at the sudden change in her attitude.

"Of course, he's right here." Mrs. Hunter handed him the phone. "It's Lily. Behave yourself."

"Hello," he said sharply.

"Hi."

Lily's voice sounded hesitant, almost shy. His anger melted away. He sat down in his chair. "Sorry I haven't called. I've been busy."

"That's okay. I understand." Her tone told him she really did understand. She knew he'd been pouting.

"What can I do for you, Lily?"

She laughed. "Funny you should ask. It's time."

"Time?" Aware that his secretary was standing nearby, he swiveled his chair around to face the windows. "Time for what?"

"My temperature's busting right off the chart, Eric. Now's the best time for your donation."

"Now? You said in two weeks." He reached for his desk calendar. "That's not for another four days."

"We're dealing with Mother Nature, Eric. Not a court docket," she said, her voice indignant.

Eric held his hand over the mouthpiece and looked at his secretary. "Isn't there a letter or something you can type?"

"If you want some privacy, Eric, all you have to do is say so." Mrs. Hunter turned on her heel, muttering.

Eric winced at the colorful language coming from his secretary's mouth. When the door closed behind her, he returned the phone to his ear. "Lily, be reasonable. I've got to be at a deposition in less than an hour."

"What are you saying, Eric? You've changed your mind?"

"No, I'm not saying that at all," he lied. Since agreeing to be a sperm donor, second thoughts seemed to loom over him. He released a slow, resigned breath. "Look, I'll see if I can work something out."

"Are you sure?"

"Yes, I'm sure," he said, feeling his anger rise at the doubtful sound of her voice. He glanced at his watch. "I'll be at the clinic in half an hour."

Scowling, he hung up the phone. His gut instinct told him he was making a mistake. A big mistake. But he'd made Lily a promise. And he wasn't one to back down from a promise. Like it or not, he was about to become a sperm donor.

Forty-five minutes later, Eric pulled his white Porsche to a stop outside the medical building. Climbing out of the car, he shucked off his suit jacket, threw it onto the passenger seat, then strode toward the offices of the fertility clinic.

He was late. He'd had trouble coercing someone to take his place at the deposition. Luckily, he'd found an associate lawyer fresh out of law school to do him the favor. Mrs. Hunter had agreed to stay and take notes and lead the associate through the deposition.

He skidded to a stop at the clinic's front desk. The receptionist, a buxom brunette, glanced at him.

"May I help you?"

"Yes, I'm here to..." He cleared his throat. "I'm here to..." He couldn't say it. For the first time in his adult life, he was at a loss for words.

The brunette smiled. "You must be a donor."

Eric felt the heat rise on his face. He straightened his tie. "That's right."

"Have you donated before, Mr. .... ?"

He glanced over his shoulder. Only one woman, a very pregnant woman, sat in the waiting room, watching him. "Mitchell. Eric Mitchell," he said, keeping his voice low. "And no, I've never donated before."

Her smile deepened with ill-concealed amusement. She pointed a manicured finger at the group of tweedy gray chairs in the waiting room.

"Have a seat, Mr. Mitchell. Someone will be right with you."

He sat down, crossing his legs, then uncrossing them. He glanced around the waiting room and caught the curious gaze of the pregnant woman. She smiled at him. He glanced down at his empty hands, then picked up a brochure and skimmed its pages, staring blindly at the words.

He wondered if he was the only man in the entire office. He felt out of place. Worse, he felt as though he were a sperm bull on display and about to be auctioned off to the highest bidder. Promise or no promise, he had to get out of there. Brochure still in hand, he stood.

"Eric," a familiar voice called to him, stopping his hasty exit.

He whirled around. Lily, dressed in a slim blue-jean skirt and Western-style blouse, looking flushed and excited, breezed into the waiting room.

"What are you doing here?" he demanded.

She laughed, her eyes sparkling. "The same thing you are. To make a baby."

"Now? I didn't..." Remembering the pregnant woman, once again he lowered his voice. "I didn't think you'd be here until later. Don't they have to freeze it or something first?"

"Eric, didn't you read the pamphlet I gave you?"

He'd skimmed the pamphlet, then forgotten about the damn thing. He shifted uncomfortably from one foot to the other.

Lily gave him an exasperated look. "Sperm loses its potency when it's frozen. The fresher the donation, the better the chance for a successful insemination."

"Mr. Mitchell?" A husky woman's voice interrupted them. A nurse, with a curly cap of gray hair and a body that fell in one straight line from shoulders to hips, stood before them. Her horn-rimmed glasses glinted in the light as she nodded in his direction. "Are you Mr. Mitchell?"

"Yes," he said, choking on the word. His mouth felt as though it were filled with cotton.

"Come with me, please." She turned, her white shoes squeaking on the linoleum.

"What about you?" he asked Lily, reluctant to leave her side.

The nurse narrowed her gaze at Lily. "Are you the recipient?"

Lily nodded.

The nurse looked at Eric, her expression stern. "She'll have to wait out here, Mr. Mitchell. No one but the donors are allowed in the cupping room."

"Cupping room?" His chest tightened.

"It's okay, Eric," Lily said. "I've brought something to read while I wait." She dug in her handbag and withdrew a book, a thick tome, at least five hundred pages.

"Come with me, Mr. Mitchell." The nurse smiled and wagged a finger at him to follow.

The walls seemed to spin as he glanced around the waiting room. The pregnant woman and the receptionist stared at him with frank, curious gazes. The nurse gave him a doubtful look, as though she expected him to take off running like a scared jackrabbit. The thought had crossed his mind. If he was smart, he would walk out the front door and never stop.

His reeling gaze ended with Lily.

Lily. She stood motionless before him, the sparkle gone from her eyes, her expression guarded. The last time he'd seen that look on her face had been three years ago—at David's funeral. Guilt washed over him. He dropped his gaze to the brochure in his hand. For the first time since picking it up, he read its title, "You and your Baby." How could he live with himself if he disappointed Lily now?

He raised his eyes, grinned at Lily, then turned to follow the surprised nurse.

Twenty minutes later, when Lily spotted Eric strolling down the corridor to rejoin her, she had already made up her mind. Eric's stint as a sperm donor would be a one-shot deal, so to speak.

He'd promised her that guilt had nothing to do with the reason he'd agreed to be a donor. But he'd lied. She'd seen that as plain as the blush on his cheeks. Guilt was the only reason Eric had agreed to help her.

Where would it stop? Would guilt prod Eric to play the doting father to her as-yet-to-be-conceived child? She shivered at the thought. Men, fathers in particular, didn't last very long in her family. She couldn't risk letting anyone, especially Eric, get that involved in her life.

Eric sat down in the seat next to her. His smile seemed a little too bright, a little too forced.

"I've got this craving for a cigarette, and I don't even smoke."

"Eric, you don't have to joke. I know how hard this was for you."

His grin was wicked. "Hard wasn't the half of it, Lily."

A hot blush stained her cheeks. She glanced around the now-crowded waiting room. "Eric, stop it, or we're going to get thrown out of the clinic."

He leaned closer. "Come on, Lily," he said, his voice low and teasing, sending shivers down her spine. "Tell me the truth. You're curious about what went on back there, aren't you?"

She raised her chin. "If handling an embarrassing situation by joking about it makes you feel better, then by all means, go right ahead."

"I knew it." He chuckled. "You're dying to know what really happened."

She exhaled slowly through clenched teeth.

"Don't worry." He winked. "I'll tell you. First, the nurse took me to this room. A small room, gray walls, tiled floor, a comfortable chair. These people really go out of their way to make you feel at home. In fact, I felt comfortable enough to be in my mother's family room." He thought about this for a moment. "Except there aren't any pictures of naked women on Mom's walls."

Lily didn't dare comment. Sometimes it was hard to tell whether Eric was serious or not.

He shook his head. "Mom's got a couple of velvet pictures of Elvis. But definitely no naked women."

Her mother had taught her an appreciation of fine art. The mention of velvet pictures and Elvis in the same breath grated on her sensitive ears. Suddenly she realized how little she knew about Eric's family. Hoping she didn't sound snobbish, she asked, "Your mother has velvet pictures of Elvis in her family room?"

He smiled, amused by her surprise. "Don't worry, Lily. It isn't genetic. Not one of my sisters or I have a weakness for Elvis."

She felt as though the breath had been knocked out of her. "You have sisters?"

"Four of them."

"Four! You never told me you had sisters," she said, her tone almost an accusation. A new picture, a more intimate picture of Eric, formed in her mind. Eric with a family. Four sisters and a mother who collected Elvis memorabilia.

He shrugged. "Didn't I?"

"No, you didn't." She couldn't shake the growing panic in her voice. She'd known Eric for almost five years, they'd been good friends for the past three. How could he forget to tell her something so important? How could she have neglected to ask?

He frowned. "I guess I forgot."

"Forgot?"

"I've always made it a policy to keep my personal life separate from my business life," he said, fidgeting in his chair.

"Oh? What am I? Business or personal?"

"Neither," he said quickly. Too quickly. "You're... different."

Different? What was that supposed to mean? She studied him, trying to decide whether she should be flattered or insulted. She decided not to think about it.

"Do you have any brothers?" she asked, pushing away the remnants of irritation.

"Nope. I'm the only boy after four girls." He grinned. "I guess my parents decided to quit while they were ahead."

Eric's good humor was contagious. She couldn't help but smile. "Your father must have felt outnumbered by all those girls. I'm sure he was relieved when you came along."

For a long moment, Eric said nothing. "I'm not really sure." His voice softened. "Dad died when I was ten."

Her smile faded. "I'm sorry."

"There's no need to be sorry. It happened a long time ago."

From the dismissive tone of his voice, Lily could tell Eric wanted to drop the subject. She slumped against the back of her chair, her head reeling with this new insight into Eric's life.

They had more in common than she'd realized. They had both lost parents. Though she knew her sympathy would be unwanted, she felt her heart go out to him. Eric's loss seemed much worse than hers. She'd never known her father. Eric had had ten years to get to know and love his. The pain must have been unbearable.

She steered the conversation to safer ground. "Youngest of five. After four girls, no less. I guess that explains a lot."

"Explains what?"

"The way you act around women."

He frowned. "Exactly how do I act around women?"

"You're a charmer, Eric. I've never seen you at a loss for words around a woman."

He chuckled. "My sisters would love to hear that. They used to worry about me, think I was too quiet."

"You? Quiet?" She smiled.

"With four girls in the house, it was hard to get a word in edgewise."

Four girls. Four aunts her child would never know. Second thoughts gripped her, shaking her resolve. After all the trouble Eric had just gone to on her behalf, she couldn't change her mind now. Could she?

Seemingly oblivious to her bout with indecision, Eric glanced around the room. "What are we waiting for now?"

"They have to determine whether your sample is good enough."

"Good enough?" He looked offended.

"They're doing a sperm count. If it's too low, they'll have to reject your donation."

He straightened in his chair. "I doubt if that'll be a problem."

Eagerly her mind snatched at the possibility. If Eric's sperm didn't pass the test, there was still a way out of this tenuous situation. "Then there's the motility rate."

"The what?"

"They check to see if they're good swimmers or not."

"You didn't tell me they'd be rating me," he said, his expression defensive.

Lily bit down the urge to smile.

Their eyes met and held. One second, two seconds, three... They burst into hoots of laughter, gut-hugging laughter that brought tears to their eyes.

Despite being the center of attention in the crowded waiting room, Lily was glad to be laughing. She hadn't realized how wound up she was until she felt the tension slip from her muscles.

After a moment, she fell back into her chair, wiping a tear from the corner of her eye. "I don't know how long the lab will take. There's no need for you to stay, Eric. I know how busy you are at the office."

"I'll wait. I'd like to know if I have to go through this again."

Her heart skipped a beat. Eric's jokes to cover his embarrassment, her insight into his family, their laughter at a most inappropriate time, all confirmed her decision. She and Eric couldn't go through this again. The emotional risks were too great.

"Mrs. Gerard." Cold panic engulfed her. The husky voice sounded all too familiar. This time the nurse was calling for her. "We're ready for you."

"So soon?" Her voice broke.

"The lab's finished?" Eric asked.

The nurse nodded. "Finished and has given a thumbs-up."

A pleased smile touched Eric's face. "How was the sperm count?"

The nurse glanced at the file in her hand. "Well over sixty million, Mr. Mitchell. Strong swimmers. Smart, too. They all seem to be heading in the right direction."

Lily's hopes for a last-minute reprieve were dashed. She should have known. Even Eric's sperm were perfect.

The decision was hers. Should she go through with the procedure or not? Her throat tightened. She swallowed hard at the rising panic.

The chance for a successful insemination the first time around was slim, she reminded herself. A pang of longing filled her. She wanted that chance. She wanted a baby. This would be her only opportunity to try. She wouldn't ask Eric to be a donor again.

Lily's legs felt like jelly as she forced herself to stand.

Eric stood, also. He reached out, his fingers encircling her wrist, stopping her. His hand felt warm against her cool skin. She shivered at his touch.

Concern filled his eyes. "Do you want me to wait?"

She hated the thought of going through this alone. But, once before, she'd made the mistake of allowing a man to become too close. Memories of David's death flooded her mind. A dull pain thumped in her chest. She'd learned the hard way; she couldn't allow herself to depend upon any man. Eric had to leave.

She shook her head. "No, this will take a while."

"I don't mind waiting."

"The insemination could take a couple of hours. Go on, Eric. Your part is over."

He seemed reluctant to leave. "Will you call me— later?"

"I'll call." She forced a smile. "Don't worry. I'll be fine."

He nodded. Then with a frown he turned on his heel.

Lily watched him leave until she heard the sound of someone clearing her throat.

"Ready?" The nurse smiled reassuringly.

She'd been more than ready when she'd arrived. Now she wasn't so sure. Lily straightened her shoulders and stood tall, hoping she looked more confident than she felt. "I'm ready."

Fate and her family's curse had taken David away from her before she'd been able to have a child, leaving a lonely void in her life. Now, with Eric's help, fate would have to decide whether she'd be given a second chance.

Eric paused at the front entrance of the clinic. He rested his hand on the bar that opened the door, feeling the cold metal against his skin. He remembered how cold Lily's skin had felt to his touch. But, unlike the metal beneath his hand, Lily had trembled.

Was she having second thoughts?

He glanced over his shoulder, catching a glimpse of Lily as she followed the nurse down the hall. She looked scared, uncertain and so alone.

At first he'd balked at the prospect of Lily waiting for him outside the cupping room. But when he returned and saw her face, her beautiful, welcoming face, she seemed heaven-sent in the middle of a hell of a lot of confusion. She'd been his calming strength. And now she wanted him to leave.

He tightened his grip on the bar. She'd told him his part was over. In his heart, he knew that she shouldn't be alone. Sometimes Lily was just too stubborn for her own good.

He spun around and returned to the waiting room, settling himself into the chair Lily had recently occupied. Lily's perfume, the scent of wildflowers, hung in the air. He breathed deeply, feeling as though a part of her were still there.

Lily would probably be angry when she found him in the waiting room when she returned. Probably use that damn curse, the one she'd tried to convince him had killed David, as an excuse.

He could weather Lily's temper. He was certain he was doing the right thing. Lily needed a friend to stand by her. And he was going to be that friend.

Chapter Three

"Lily, phone call. Dr. Glaser's office," Ann, Lily's assistant, informed her.

Lily jumped. In her hand, she held a pastry bag filled with icing. With one miscalculated squeeze, the intricate cascade of flowers she'd been designing turned into a blob of white.

Lily closed her eyes, counted to ten and struggled to regain her composure. She opened one eye at a time and peeked at the mess. It looked worse than she had first thought.

Ann, a tall, willowy blonde, stood next to her, studying the cake. Then she swung her curious gaze to Lily. "You okay, Lily?"

"I'm fine. See what you can do with this mess." Lily handed Ann the pastry bag. "Please?"

Lily picked up a wet towel and wiped her sticky fingers as she hurried to the office. This morning, two weeks after the insemination, she'd gone back to the fertility clinic for a pregnancy test. Dr. Glaser had promised to call her with the results in the afternoon. Now she was about to find out whether she was pregnant.

Not bothering to close the door, she hurried to the phone. "Hello."

"Mrs. Gerard?" a woman asked.

"Yes," she said. Her voice sounded breathless, more from excitement than from the rush into her office.

"Please hold for Dr. Glaser."

A click sounded, then Muzak with a Latin beat filtered over the phone line. Her pounding heart kept time with the pulsing brass horns. Lily took a deep breath, trying to calm her strained nerves.

In midnote the Muzak stopped.

"Mrs. Gerard, this is Dr. Glaser."

Lily's throat felt as though it had closed up on her. "Hi," she said breathlessly.

"Looks as though we've had a successful insemination. Congratulations, Lily. You're going to have a baby."

"A baby," she repeated, her voice filled with wonderment. Her legs gave out beneath her. She dropped her backside onto the top of her desk.

"You're a lucky lady." Dr. Glaser's deep chuckle filled her ears. "Not many people hit a homer first time at bat."

Lucky lady. Lily couldn't help but smile. She wondered what Dr. Glaser would say if he knew the truth, if he knew just how *unlucky* a lady she really was.

"Once you've had time to adjust to the news, give my receptionist a call," he said. "She'll set up an appointment for your first checkup." He paused. "I'm glad everything went so smoothly."

Her smile deepened. "Thank you, Dr. Glaser."

Feeling almost light-headed, she hung up the phone. Gently she pressed a hand to her stomach. Until this moment, she'd refused to consider the possibility that the insemination had worked, that she had conceived. In less than nine months, she would have a baby.

Eric. She reached for the phone. She had to call Eric.

She stopped, her hand resting on the receiver. Eric had waited over two hours for her at the clinic the day of the insemination. Her chest tightened as she recalled the anger she'd felt when she'd walked into the lobby and found him still there. Not angry at Eric, but angry with herself. She had been so relieved he hadn't left.

Lily sighed. When she had asked Eric to be a sperm donor, she assumed he'd pay a passing interest in what was happening. Since the insemination, he'd showered her with phone calls, dinner invitations, visits to the bakery—all under the guise of friendship. But she knew the truth. He was checking up on her.

Why did he have to be so caring? So considerate? Why did she have to enjoy the unexpected attention? Now she couldn't wait to tell him the news that she was pregnant with his child.

Not *his* child.

Her child.

She dropped her hand from the phone. Lily recalled the day she'd learned of the curse. The day she'd turned thirteen and had been curious about the lack of men in her life. She'd been foolish enough to scoff at her mother's tale of a family curse. When she'd married David, she was determined to prove her mother wrong. Pain pressed against her heart. She'd learned the hard way that she would never have the perfect storybook family. A husband, a father for her child, wasn't in her future.

In the past few years and especially these past few weeks, she'd come to depend on Eric. His humor, his wit, his company all filled a void in her life. But she was allowing herself to become much too close to him. She wasn't being fair to Eric or to herself.

She stared at the phone.

She would have to tell him the news. But she'd also make it clear his involvement in her pregnancy was over. She'd made the decision to raise her baby on her own. Now it was up to her to see that she stuck with that decision.

Seven o'clock that evening, Eric sat at his office desk, making a final check on a legal brief. At the credenza across the room, his secretary, Mrs. Hunter, was busy sorting through documents to file. The phone rang. Mrs. Hunter turned, her hands filled with papers.

Eric shook his head. "I've got it." He reached for the phone. "Eric Mitchell."

"Answering your own phone? Has anyone ever told you, you work too hard?"

Adam smiled, recognizing the caller's voice. "Only my mother and a pesky redhead have had the nerve."

He leaned back in his chair and listened to the sound of Lily's laughter.

"If I ever meet your mother, remind me to commend her on her good sense."

"I will." Eric ran a finger over the file on his desk, recalling the last time Lily had called him at the office, the day he'd gone to the fertility clinic and become a sperm donor. "What can I do for you, Lily?"

He listened as Lily took a deep breath.

Eric inhaled slowly, waiting.

"I went to the clinic today for a pregnancy test."

"And?"

"The results were positive. I'm pregnant."

He exhaled, giving himself a moment to cope with the flood of mixed emotions before answering. Lily had told him the chances of a successful insemination the first try were slim. A smile touched his lips. He felt an unexpected rush of pure male pride. Guess there was no question now—his sperm certainly was good enough.

Macho pride aside, Lily was pregnant. All the pamphlets in the world couldn't have prepared him for the shock. He wondered what the appropriate response was for a sperm donor who had just found out he had successfully impregnated a donee.

He frowned. To hell with etiquette. This was Lily. His best friend. Nothing, not even a pregnancy, would change a relationship as strong as theirs.

"That's great," he said finally, forcing a casual tone. "Just great. We should go out and celebrate. Have you eaten? I'll take you out for dinner."

"No." Lily's blunt refusal vibrated in his ear. "I've had a busy day. I'm really bushed."

"How about tomorrow night?"

"Tomorrow's Friday, Eric. The start of the weekend. It's one of the bakery's busiest days."

He felt a twinge of irritation. For whatever reason, Lily was putting him off. Maybe she was embarrassed, he told himself. They'd been through a very intimate experience. As intimate an experience two people can have short of being lovers. Regaining the comfortable footing of their old friendship might be harder than he thought.

Maybe she just needed time alone to adjust to the news. He should drop the subject and give her the time she needed, but he hated taking no for an answer. "The bakery's closed on Sunday. We'll celebrate then."

"I've already made plans for Sunday. I'm sorry, Eric." Before he could say another word, she continued, "Look,

I'll call you sometime next week. We'll make plans then. Bye."

Eric stared at the phone in his hand. Irritation latched onto his tumultuous mood like a prickly burr. Before, he'd only thought Lily was trying to avoid him. Now, he was sure of it. When a woman called to tell him he'd made her pregnant, the last thing he expected was a brush-off. He slammed the phone back onto its cradle.

Mrs. Hunter jumped. "My goodness, Eric. You've got to learn to take no a little more gracefully."

He'd forgotten his secretary was still in his office. She'd been a witness to the entire conversation. A hot flush of embarrassment warmed his face. "Aren't you finished yet?" he growled.

"Lily's certainly put you in a fine mood. Anything wrong?"

His secretary had signed the consent form. She was the only person he'd told that he'd agreed to be a sperm donor. Who was he kidding? She was the only person he would *ever* tell. Maybe she could help him understand Lily.

"She's pregnant," he admitted.

Mrs. Hunter stared at him for a long moment. "Well, congratulations. You're going to be a daddy."

He rose to his feet, his chair spinning out behind him. "No, Lily's going to be a mommy."

"I see," she said, raising one brow. "That's why you're in such a *good* mood? Because you're *not* going to be a daddy?"

Frustrated, he slammed his fisted hands into his pants pockets and crossed to the windows. He stared out at the dusky sky.

"Eric, did you ever wonder why Lily asked you to be a donor?"

He frowned, turning away from the windows. "What do you mean?"

Mrs. Hunter shrugged. "She could have had an anonymous donor. I find it curious that she went to the trouble of asking you to be the father."

"If you're insinuating there's something between Lily and me, you're wrong. She was married to David. We're just good friends."

"Good friends who have something more than a death in common. Now you have a baby."

Her words had a stunning effect. He felt as though the air had been knocked from his lungs.

She smiled patiently. "Eric, did you really expect your friendship with Lily not to change?"

He took a deep breath. "I don't know what I expected. She needed my help—"

"And you certainly did help. Now she's pushing you away."

"That's the way it seems." He glanced back at the windows. "Do you think I made a mistake?"

"Not yet you haven't."

The emphatic tone of his secretary's voice surprised him. "I'm glad one of us is sure." He shook his head. "What am I supposed to do now?"

"You're a smart man, Eric. You figure it out." Mrs. Hunter turned on her heel and strode to the door. "Go home, Eric. It's late."

"Now she gives me advice," he muttered as the office door clicked shut behind his secretary.

He glanced out the window. The sun had almost bade its final farewell. The circle of light from his desk lamp fell short of the window, leaving him in the shadow of darkness. He'd never felt so confused or so alone.

He clenched his hands into fists of frustration. He wanted to go over to Lily's and shake some sense into that stubborn head of hers. She was pregnant. How could she push him away at a time when she needed him the most?

Slowly he unclenched his fingers. Maybe it was time he admitted the truth. A part of him was relieved Lily didn't want to put the burden of parenthood on his shoulders. He hadn't asked to be a father. And as far as he knew, his being a father was the last thing Lily wanted.

Obviously she didn't want to see him. Maybe he should give her some time. Let things cool down for a couple of days. Then see how she felt. If she still didn't want his help, then fine. He'd have given it his best shot. Lily would be a single parent. He had to respect her wishes.

Eric stared blindly into the night. So why did he feel so lousy?

He sat down in his chair, opened a desk drawer and withdrew a file marked Personal. He riffled through the pages until he came across his copy of the donor consent form. Minutes slowly slipped away as he stared at the document in his hand.

When he'd signed the consent form, he'd had the nerve to think of himself as noble. He'd told himself he was helping a friend in need. He scowled. Nobility—fairy-tale fluff. Contracts were his field of expertise. He'd gone over the consent form with a microscope, making sure that his best interests were being protected.

He tossed the form onto his desk. He'd signed away all parental rights and responsibilities without a moment's hesitation. It looked good on paper. But once again, it was time for a reality check. Thanks to him, a child had been conceived. A child who would never know his father.

He'd spent most of his life without the love and care of a father. How could he have sentenced his child to the same fate?

Saturday, the bakery's biggest business day of the week, and Lily felt as though she were moving in slow motion. She refused to attribute her lethargy to her pregnancy.

She blamed Eric.

Two days had passed without a word from him. But he'd never strayed far from her mind. During the waking hours, she'd found herself jumping every time the phone rang or the doorbell chimed, wondering if it was Eric. At night, thoughts of him left her too restless to sleep. She'd spent most of last night tossing and turning in her bed. A part of her wished she hadn't been so brusque with him the last time they'd talked. But another part wondered if she'd been blunt enough. What if Eric hadn't gotten the message? What if he insisted on being a father to her child?

Despite the oppressive heat of the kitchen, Lily shivered. She realized she was merely putting off the inevitable. This brief respite from Eric wouldn't last forever. Eventually she'd have to face him. She only wished she knew what she'd say when she did.

Thank you for your help, Eric. Now that I'm pregnant I don't ever want to see you again? Lily groaned. Her intentions may have been good. She may have been trying to spare Eric the obligations and risks involved in parenting her child, but even to her well-intentioned ears it sounded as though she were giving him the old, thankless boot.

"Lily, Mrs. Fogel, line one," Ann said, interrupting her thoughts.

Lily gave Ann a tired nod. She wiped a hand across her forehead. Her skin felt cold and clammy to the touch even though the kitchen was hot. She should have worn a dress, not slacks. The cotton fabric was sticking to her legs like a second skin. She took a deep breath and inhaled the cloying sweetness of icing and freshly baked cakes that permeated the air. A bitter taste filled her mouth. Lily struggled to control a bout of queasiness as she picked up the phone.

"Hello, Mrs. Fogel."

Mrs. Fogel was a pleasant woman who hadn't suffered the prewedding jitters Lily usually associated with mothers of the bride. But now the woman's frantic voice boomed across the phone line.

The commotion brought Ann to her side.

"Slow down, Mrs. Fogel. Which part of the wedding cake is missing?" Lily held the phone inches away from her ear, still able to hear the words clearly.

"The top . . . with the figures of the bride and groom?"

Lily's unsteady stomach lurched. She and Ann exchanged worried glances. The Fogel wedding and reception were being held at a nearby resort in Scottsdale. The wedding was to start in less than an hour, with the reception following immediately. Time was running out. Ann began a search of the kitchen.

Lily turned her attention to soothing the woman on the phone. "Don't worry, Mrs. Fogel. We'll find the cake. No, I'm not sure how this happened."

Lily pressed a hand to her tummy. She'd been in charge of the Fogel cake. She'd supervised its preparation and loading. If part of the cake was missing, she had no one to blame but herself. The thought of her own carelessness ruining a bride's special day made her feel worse.

Ann disappeared into the showroom. Seconds later, Lily heard a triumphant whoop. Ann returned to the kitchen holding the cake. Lily drew in a shaky breath. From the groom in his shiny black tux to the bride in her white net dress, the cake looked perfect.

"Mrs. Fogel, we found the cake. It'll be there in ten minutes."

While she apologized for the mix-up, Ann packed the cake and sent it on its way with the delivery boy. Lily replaced the phone on its cradle, breathing a sigh of relief. Unfortunately, her relief hadn't caught up with the rest of her body. Her stomach still churned. She felt oddly lightheaded. She pulled up a stool and sat down hard. Closing her eyes, she asked, "Where was it?"

"Someone put it in the front showroom," Ann said, concern edging her voice. "You don't look so good, Lily."

Leaning her elbows on the counter, Lily rubbed her throbbing temples. "I'll be fine. I just need a moment to collect myself."

The front door chimed the arrival of a customer.

Lily moaned.

"You keep sitting," Ann said. "I'll handle the customer."

On Saturdays, Lily divided her time between decorating cakes, sending the finished products off to various receptions and meeting with prospective clients. Usually she handled the job with ease, thriving on the fast, hectic pace. But today her energy level had hit an all-time low. She slumped a notch lower in her seat. She couldn't wait for the day to be over.

Then Lily heard Eric's deep voice. She forced her eyes open.

When David had died, Eric had been there with a strong shoulder for her to lean on. Now, with her feeling sick and tired, that shoulder seemed awful tempting. She gave herself a mental shake. What was wrong with her? The last thing she needed was for Eric to see her languishing like a flower in the desert heat. In front of him, she needed to be healthy, full of pep and vigor, or he'd never believe she could handle this pregnancy alone. She jumped off the stool.

Her first mistake.

Taking a step was her next.

"Oh, no," she moaned, feeling the room spin beneath her feet. Her muscles went as limp as a rag doll's. She grabbed for the counter, but missed. Then, expecting to hit the tiled floor, she felt herself being swept away into a pair of strong arms.

"Lily." Eric's voice rumbled in her ear.

She wanted to answer, but couldn't. She pried open her eyes. The room blurred, making her feel as though she were watching a movie out of focus.

"It's too hot in here." Eric sounded worried.

"The Wedding Alcove's cooler." Ann's voice penetrated the fog.

They were moving now.

"Put me down, Eric," she murmured, resting her face against the solid strength of his shoulder. His shirt felt soft, the skin beneath warm. She wished the dizziness would end.

His chest rose and fell sharply. "She's arguing," he said, cradling her tight. "She'll be okay."

"I'll get some water," Ann said.

The wicker love seat creaked as he lowered her onto its cushions. After Eric released her, he stepped back. A rush of cool air bathed her skin. The breeze felt heavenly, but she missed the security of his arms. Lily flopped her head back against the cushions, closed her eyes and told her body to relax.

"Put your head between your legs," Eric said, his tone brisk.

She opened an eye and squinted at him. He was down on one knee before her, and she saw the deep lines of concern that etched his face. The look was almost her undoing. She felt the sharp sting of tears press against her eyes as a confusing mixture of emotions collided in her mind.

She had never fainted before. Fainting scared her. Being unable to control what was happening to her body left her feeling vulnerable. It felt good having someone fuss over her. For just a moment, she didn't want to be strong. She wanted to be pampered, protected.

Lily pushed these feelings aside. She couldn't admit vulnerability to Eric or even to herself. If she acknowledged she needed his help, she'd be giving up her independence. She couldn't allow Eric to feel a sense of responsibility toward her or her baby.

She closed her eyes and squeezed out his caring image. "I don't want to put my head between my legs. I'm fine just the way I am."

"Jeez, you're cranky when you're sick."

"I'm not sick," she said. "I'm just a little light-headed."

"Light-headed? You were about to kiss the floor when I walked in."

Slowly she opened her eyes. Her head still felt fuzzy, but at least the room had stopped spinning. "Kiss the floor?"

"It's too damn hot in that kitchen. And I bet you were trying to do ten things at once." He released a terse breath. "You're pregnant, Lily. Your body's trying to tell you to slow down."

No one but Eric knew of her pregnancy. She shot a wary glance toward the showroom and kitchen. "Why don't you just announce it to the world, Eric?"

He lowered his voice, but his frustration rang loud and clear. "You need a watchdog. Someone who'll make sure you're taking care of yourself."

Lily groaned. She wasn't feeling up to this argument. "I can take care of myself."

Ann breezed in, carrying a glass of water. She glanced from one to the other, taking in their stormy expressions. With a thin smile, she handed Eric the water. "I'll go tell everyone you're all right, Lily."

Ann backed out of the alcove.

Eric gave the glass to Lily, his handsome face drawn into stern lines.

She took a sip. The fuzziness was subsiding. Along with a clearer head came the realization that maybe she was being a bit ungracious. "Look, Eric, I'm glad you were here to catch me when I got a little off-balance. Thank you for your concern."

"You scared ten years off my life, and all you can say is thanks for my concern?" He narrowed his eyes. "Until this baby is born, I'm going to make sure you're taking care of yourself. Consider this your first and only warning. For the rest of your pregnancy, I'm going to be your guilty conscience and guardian angel all rolled up in one."

Her worries of sounding ungrateful disappeared. A slow burn of irritation took their place. "You want to be my guardian angel?"

He nodded.

"Guardian angels are for children, Eric," she said, holding a loose rein on her growing anger.

"Children and adults who obviously can't take care of themselves," he retorted, his tone matter-of-fact.

She tightened her grip around the glass. It took all of her willpower not to throw its contents into Eric's smug face. To think she'd wasted all that time worrying about being rude. "You feel I can't take care of myself? That I'm worse than a child?"

"I didn't say that."

"But you're implying—"

He raised a brow. "Well, if the image fits . . ."

Her control snapped. "Of all the macho, arrogant—"

"Now, Lily."

His placating tone proved to be the final straw. Anger kicked in. Lily placed the glass on the wicker table, moving it away from temptation. She folded her hands in her lap, took a deep breath and told Eric exactly what he could do with his guilty conscience and aspirations of being an angel.

Chapter Four

Six o'clock that evening the doorbell rang. Lily glanced out the living-room window. A four-foot stuffed panda and Eric stood on her front step.

Lily groaned.

Earlier that afternoon, Eric had stormed out of the bakery. In a show of anger, he'd slammed the glass door behind him and knocked the door chime from its perch. Her immediate reaction to his hotheaded antics had been self-righteous indignation. But once her light-headedness had passed and she'd had the entire afternoon to mull over their conversation, her temper had cooled.

She realized she'd been a bit harsh. After all, Eric was her friend. It was only natural for him to worry about her. She peered out her window again and frowned. However, his concern did border on high-handed male chauvinism.

"You might as well open up, Lily." Eric's voice filtered through the door's oak panels. "You know I won't leave until you do."

His remark conjured memories of another time, another confrontation. After David had died, she'd holed up in her house and refused to see anyone. Eric had given her seven days of self-imposed isolation. Then he'd had enough. On that bright-and-sunny seventh day, he'd camped out on her doorstep. For more than two hours, he'd carried on a one-sided conversation through a closed door, refusing to budge until she finally let him in. He hadn't let her push him away then, and he wouldn't allow her to do it now.

Lily sighed. Damn, but the man was stubborn.

She glanced at her oversize yellow T-shirt, the white cotton leggings and her bare feet. She was dressed for comfort, not for receiving guests. She narrowed her eyes. But, then again, Eric was an uninvited guest.

She swung open the door.

Eric shot her a wary glance. "You aren't going to cuss at me again, are you?"

Her cheeks burned with embarrassment. "Are you here to provoke me?"

"No, ma'am. I learned my lesson this afternoon." He grinned. "The hard way."

Her resolve to send him and his bear packing melted under a pair of warm brown eyes. She collapsed against the doorframe. What was wrong with her? Why couldn't she stay mad at him?

She tore her eyes away from Eric and glanced at the panda. "Who's your friend?"

"He doesn't have a name yet," Eric said. "Since he's yours, I thought you'd like to have the honors."

"Mine?"

"Well, the baby's." His grin was sheepish. "I wanted to be the first to give him a gift."

"Her," she murmured, bracing herself against the warm fuzzy feeling that threatened to envelop her. She was dangerously close to falling under Eric's charm.

"Excuse me?"

"The baby—it's a girl."

He frowned. "How do you know?"

"I just do." She gave herself a mental shake. Don't let him distract you with talk about the baby. Concentrate, she told herself. Eric had to leave. "Eric, this was sweet of you. But I'm very tired. I'm not up to a visit."

"I won't stay long," he persisted. "We need to talk."

Her gaze was wary. "About what?"

He shifted his grip around the panda's neck. "It's hot out here. Couldn't we talk inside?"

"About what, Eric?"

He sighed. "About us. About the baby. Avoiding each other isn't going to make the problem go away."

She raised her chin defiantly. "I didn't realize we had a problem."

He gave her an incredulous look. "How can you say that after what happened this afternoon?"

"Nothing happened," she lied.

His mouth curved into a grin. "Watch it, Lily. Keep lying and your nose is going to start growing."

She glared at him.

"Are you going to let me in or not?"

Reluctantly, she stepped aside, allowing him to enter. A jumble of arms and elbows passed her in the tiny foyer, one pair soft and fuzzy, one pair hard and strong. A hand grazed her breasts as the duo slipped by. Lily sucked in a surprised breath. No doubt about it. Those fingers belonged to a man. There was nothing soft or fuzzy about the tingling sensation the accidental touch set off in her body.

"Where do you want him?" he asked, indicating the bear.

"Leave him at the door." Lily's gaze traveled from the panda to Eric. "I'm not sure if he's staying."

Eric chuckled as he dropped the bear at her feet. He wore a tropical shirt, khaki shorts and Docksiders without socks. He looked flushed. Perspiration dampened his forehead.

"It sure is hot outside." He heaved a sigh. "Yep, wrestling with a teddy bear works up a thirst." He raised a brow. "I guess asking for a drink would be out of the question?"

She gave a long-suffering sigh, turned on her heel and headed for the kitchen. "I have orange juice, water or cola."

"Water's fine."

His voice sounded close. Too close.

She grabbed a glass out of the cupboard and filled it with ice and water from a pitcher in the refrigerator. Out of the corner of her eye, she watched as Eric settled himself at her kitchen table. The massive bleached-oak table and chairs matched the tall, lean proportions of his body. He slouched low in his seat, stretching his long legs and making himself comfortable. With one arm resting on the tabletop, the other on the back of his chair, he looked like a man at ease with his surroundings.

A man who felt at home.

The image sent butterflies dancing in her stomach. She and David bought this house when they'd first married. David had lived there only a few months, not nearly long enough to call it home. Now Eric was settling himself in as though he belonged, painting a disturbing picture of history about to repeat itself.

A shiver of apprehension traveled down her spine. No man belonged in her home, she told herself sternly, especially not Eric.

"What do you want, Eric?" she demanded. She handed him the glass, their fingers brushing. His touch felt warm, strong and anything but reassuring. She hoped he wouldn't notice the way her hand shook.

Scowling, he shifted his grip, allowing her to drop her hand. "I want you to stop acting as prickly as a cactus and start acting like my friend again."

Lily sat in a chair opposite Eric. "Are you sure that's all you want to be? Just a friend?"

He looked confused. "I don't understand."

"Don't you?" She hesitated, searching for the right words. "Bringing the baby a gift was kind of you. But I don't want you to get the wrong idea."

"What idea might that be?" A tiny vein on the side of his neck pulsed a warning.

Taking a deep breath of determination, she said, "Eric, I don't need a father for this child."

"Who said I wanted to be a father?"

Lily squirmed in her chair. "No one, but I need—"

"You need . . ." The glass hit the table with a thump. Water splattered onto the tabletop.

Startled, Lily looked at Eric. Fiery anger lit his eyes. In all the years she'd known him, she'd never seen Eric lose his temper. Until today, that is. Today he'd lost his temper twice.

"Since I agreed to be a sperm donor, all I've been hearing about is what you need. Have you ever once considered what I might need?"

Lily opened her mouth to answer. Then closed it with a click, too stunned to speak.

He continued, "Or maybe my needs are last on your list of concerns. After all, you got what you wanted from me—my donation. Now that you're pregnant, I'm expendable." He narrowed his eyes. "There are terms for the way I feel, Lily. *Used* is just one of them."

"Used?" Her mouth dropped open in surprise. "I've never used a man in my life."

"Oh, yeah?" His frown deepening, he leaned back in his chair. "Well, it sure feels like it to me."

The weight of guilt pressed against her heart as she considered his accusation. She'd never viewed herself as a selfish person. But after listening to Eric, she felt greedy and opportunistic. "I'm sorry, Eric. I never expected you to feel so strongly about this," she said, wincing inwardly at the weak-sounding apology.

"What did you expect, Lily? As soon as I found out you were pregnant I'd start avoiding you? You know me better than that." He took a deep breath, the lines of tension easing from his face. "Look, I'm not saying I want to be your baby's father."

She raised her chin a notch, meeting his gaze. "That's the way it sounds to me."

A look of pure frustration crossed his face. "I just want to be your friend. You're alone in Phoenix, Lily. I want to be someone you can rely on. Someone to help you through the next nine months."

His offer was tempting. When she'd called with the news of her pregnancy, her mother had insisted on moving back to Phoenix for the winter months, until after the baby was born. Though she'd been grateful for the offer, Lily had refused. Her mother and grandmother hated living in the city. They thrived in the quiet beauty of

Sedona's Oak Creek Canyon. She couldn't allow them to uproot their lives for her sake. Now Eric was offering his friendship; he was someone she could rely on if she needed help.

She pushed the thought away, remembering her resolve to keep Eric safely out of her life. "Don't you think I'd like that, too?"

He gave a growl of impatience. "Then why are we arguing about this? Let me help you."

"I wish I could, but I can't." She shook her head. "I don't have a choice. Believe me, it's for your own good."

Like a light, understanding dawned on his face. "Wait a minute. Are you talking about that curse?"

"Of course I am. What did you think?"

Eric stared at her for a full minute. Then he grinned, chuckling softly. "The last excuse I expected to hear from you was that crazy curse of yours."

"Crazy curse?"

He sobered, trying to appear innocent. "Did I say crazy? I meant curious."

"Eric, it's time for you to go." She scrambled to her feet.

The chair rasped against the tiled floor as he stood. His hands gripped her shoulders, turning her to face him. The smile had faded, but amusement still lit his eyes.

"Let's try to reason through this problem, Lily. I'm sure if we put our heads together we can come up with a solution. Now, this alleged curse of yours—"

She stepped back, forcing him to release her. "Alleged?"

"Okay, scratch alleged. This curse of yours kills off any man you marry. Do lovers count, too?" He frowned. "Has there been anyone else? I mean, other than David?"

She let out an impatient breath. "Are you asking me, have I had other lovers? Or have I killed anyone else?"

"I . . . umm."

It was her turn to smile as he struggled with an answer. Seeing someone as unflappable as Eric lose his composure did wonders to boost her self-confidence. She let him flounder for a few seconds before giving him a break. "The answer is no, to both questions."

An unsettling look of relief crossed his face. She wondered what it meant. Was he relieved she hadn't killed anyone else? Or that she hadn't had any other lovers?

"Then I'm in no danger," he said, breaking into her thoughts.

She frowned. "How do you figure that?"

"I'm not your lover, Lily. There's no way your curse can affect me."

"But you did father my child. In my family, fathers don't last long."

"I'm not in your family, Lily." His expression became serious. "The bottom line is this. I may be the biological father, but that doesn't make me a parent." He sighed. "I don't think I'd even know how to be a parent. All I want is to make sure you and the baby are okay. I just want to be your friend."

That warm feeling enveloped her again as Eric's charms worked their magic. Her resolve to keep him safely out of her life didn't seem so logical or so important. To tell the truth, she needed a friend.

She shot him a doubtful gaze. "I guess we could give it a try and see what happens."

He nodded, looking satisfied. "Good." Then he grinned. "So, you're pregnant, eh?"

She returned his smile. "Yes, Eric. I'm pregnant."

"Told anyone else yet?"

"Just my mother... and you," she admitted.

"Then let me be the first to congratulate you here in Phoenix. You're going to make a great mom."

He scooped her into his arms, surprising her with an impromptu hug.

A confusing flush of heat warmed her body. In her mind, she assured herself the hug was innocent, a simple display of affection from one friend to another. But her heart seemed to have leaped into her throat. She swallowed hard and wondered why all of a sudden his arms didn't feel so friendly.

"I'm going to take good care of you," he said without releasing her. "You won't regret this, Lily."

She looked up into his brown eyes and sighed. She already did.

Two weeks later, Lily stepped back and examined the cake on the reception table with a critical eye.

Months earlier, when the bride had picked out the largest, most expensive cake she made, Lily had been ecstatic. When the bride insisted Lily be there to supervise the delivery and serving of the cake, she'd been reluctant. Taking an entire Saturday out of her busy schedule just to serve a cake seemed impractical.

But Lily had an unwritten policy in dealing with brides-to-be. On her wedding day, the bride deserved to have her every dream and wish fulfilled. If she wanted the biggest, gaudiest cake money could buy, so be it. If she wanted to pay Lily extra to serve that monstrosity, then so much the better. After all, the client was always right.

The bride had told her that the wedding and reception were to be held at the groom's home. Lily assumed the house would be a typical Arizona ranch. When she'd arrived to deliver the cake, she'd realized her mistake. The large multilevel house with its endless number of steps was a caterer's nightmare. Lily had held her breath the entire way as her workers transferred the cake from the delivery van to the reception table.

For once in her life, Lady Luck seemed to have been with her. The cake had gone through the transfer without a blemish. She breathed a sigh of relief as she turned to one of her workers. "It looks perfect."

He grinned, appearing pleased by the compliment.

"Now all we need are the lights and fountain," she told him.

He motioned to his co-worker. "We'll go to the van and bring 'em in."

Lily nodded. "I'll check for the outlets."

Lily glanced at the wall behind the table. No outlet. She gritted her teeth. The bride had promised her that an electrical outlet would be within easy reach of the table. Maybe it was on the floor under the table.

She glanced down at the slender skirt of her apricot dress. She wasn't exactly dressed for crawling around on the floor. Muttering an unladylike oath, she got down on her knees, picked up one end of the eggshell-pink cloth and poked her head under the table.

Then she heard a slow, wolfish whistle.

Lily jumped, knocking her head. Rubbing her temple, she emerged from beneath the table, a scathing remark on the tip of her tongue. The remark died on her lips. She looked up to see Eric, grinning and enjoying the view.

"Even at this angle, I didn't have any trouble recognizing you. How 'ya doing, Lily," he drawled.

Lily felt a blush warm her cheeks. Eric towered over her, putting her at a disadvantage. As she stared up at him, his smile deepened. She caught a glimpse of white, even teeth. His brown eyes sparkled with a fam... of amusement.

She sat back on her heels and gave him an asses... gaze. Dressed in a wheat-colored suit and a creamy-white shirt topped with a brown silk tie, Eric appeared cool and confident. Lily gave a silent moan. She was kidding herself. He looked good enough to eat. Had he always been this handsome, this delicious? Or was she just noticing him in a different way?

She pushed the troubling thought from her mind. "If you're here for the wedding, you're about an hour too early."

"I'm not here for the wedding. Not exactly, anyway." He patted his briefcase. "Business."

"Business?" She frowned. "Eric, you've got it all mixed up. This is a wedding, not a divorce."

"We lawyers never let an opportunity slip away. Have you ever heard the term *prenuptial agreement,* Lily?"

She covered her ears with her hands. "Don't say it. Don't spoil my illusions. Since I was a little girl, I've associated weddings with one thing—love. I don't want to hear anything about contracts."

Adam tsked. "Always the romantic."

"Don't knock romantics. They keep me in business, Eric."

"And it's your disillusioned romantics that keep me in business."

Lily struggled to her feet. No small trick in her tight dress.

Eric reached out a hand. "Need some help?"

She stared at him for a moment. She wanted to slap his hand away and make it perfectly clear she was capable of taking care of herself. She bit back the urge. He's just offering his hand, she reminded herself, not a lifetime commitment of care for her or her baby.

She placed her hand in his, palm against palm. Her breath caught as his warm grip tightened and he pulled her to her feet. The quick motion threw her off-balance. She clung to him until she regained her equilibrium. Staring up into his smiling brown eyes, she realized that she was fighting a losing battle.

For the past two weeks, they'd walked a tightwire of strained emotions. They'd talked on the phone, met for an occasional lunch and pretended nothing had changed between them. They'd gone out of their way to prove they were still good friends.

They were wrong.

Despite the circumstances, together they had created a baby. An undeniably intimate bond held them. For the first time, she felt uncomfortably aware of Eric as more than just a friend. Much more. Quickly she dropped her hand.

"How have you been feeling?" he asked.

"A little queasy. A little tired." She shrugged. "Nothing I can't handle."

He nodded. "Good."

He studied her face, then dropped his glance to her flat stomach.

Without thinking, she pressed a hand to her tummy, spreading her fingers protectively.

His eyes shot up to her face. He looked flustered. "I've got to go...to collect a couple of signatures, or there won't be a wedding this afternoon."

"Then by all means go." She forced a smile, trying to keep the situation light. She gestured toward the cake. "I want to be paid for this masterpiece."

He grinned. "Right. Maybe I'll see you later?"

"Maybe," she said noncommittally.

He turned. The heels of his brown loafers clicked on the marble floors, echoing his long-legged, confident strides. Soon he disappeared from her view.

She released a shaky breath. Her head felt as though it were spinning. She leaned against the wall, a safe distance from the cake, and wondered if she'd ever be able to look Eric in the eye again and not feel as though her world were being turned upside down.

"Bob, I don't usually say this to a man minutes before he's going to be married, but have you ever considered giving up women?" Eric asked his client, a slightly bald, middle-age man, as they walked toward the living room, where the wedding was to take place. "I'm serious, Bob. This is your third trip down the aisle. And even though we've finally worked out a prenuptial agreement, this marriage is going to cost you dearly if it doesn't work out."

Bob snorted a laugh. "It's not going to cost me that much, Eric."

"Fifty-thousand dollars a year and a condo in West Palm Beach. I'd say that's a lot."

Bob stopped and peered into an extravagant, gold-plated mirror. He adjusted the points on his bow tie. "It's just money, Eric. What good is money if you don't have love?"

"I grew up without money, Bob. It wasn't all that great."

Unwanted memories crowded Eric's mind. When his father had died, his mother had been left unprepared. Unskilled and minimally educated, she had been forced to work at a low-paying job. Every day had been a constant challenge for her to make ends meet.

While his memories of childhood were happy, he'd never quite forgotten the hand-to-mouth existence that had held his family most of his growing years. The experience left him with an appreciation of the things money could buy. And an understanding of the hardships lack of money could cause.

Early in life, making money became the force that drove him. He had worked hard to put himself through college, then law school. After passing the bar, he'd pushed himself to succeed, to be the best in his field.

A brief flirtation with wedded bliss hadn't lessened his appreciation of money, as it had for his client. In fact, it had had the opposite effect. His own near brush with marriage had caused him to become protective of his bank account.

Maybe too protective?

He pushed the doubts from his mind. Lily had called him cynical. He considered himself practical. Marriage involved more than two people falling in love. It involved the merging of two different incomes, the spending of assets, the handling of retirement funds... just to name a few. If a person took on a business partner, he'd draw up a contract assuring each party of equal protection in case of disillusionment. Why not think of marriage in the same terms?

This time Lily was wrong, he told himself confidently. With his sensible approach to marriage, he'd make a great husband.

He'd make a great husband?

Eric gave his head a shake, unable to believe the direction his thoughts had taken him. He turned to his client, anxious to distance himself from the man's dangerously romantic influence. "What I think is beside the point.

What's important is that you're happy with the prenuptial agreement."

Bob slapped him on the back. "Of course I am. Now, I insist you stay for the wedding. Maybe some of my happiness will rub off on you and put you in the mood to find yourself a woman to love."

Eric's mouth went dry. He swallowed hard at the rising panic. "I'm afraid you're wasting your time. I'm too much of a skeptic to believe in the life-altering powers of love. But I will stay for the wedding."

Minutes later, Eric seated himself in the last row of chairs in the living room. The cavernous room held fifty chairs arranged into two groups, with a wide aisle down the center. As the music started, Eric glanced around.

His gaze rested briefly on the bride. The tall blonde looked elegant, cool. He recalled the weeks they had spent hammering out a prenuptial agreement. When it came to negotiations, the bride could have given a union boss a run for his money. Eric shivered, feeling as though an icy palm had been pressed against his back. He gave this marriage six—maybe seven—months tops.

His gaze wandered. On the opposite side of the room he spotted Lily. Even if he hadn't known her, she would have stood out. Not because of the apricot dress, which clung to her shapely curves. And not because of the auburn hair, which looked like burnished gold in the sunlight streaming through the windows. But because she was the only person in the room crying.

Adam watched as Lily dabbed at the tears falling from her eyes with a white, lacy handkerchief. Even at this distance, he could see that the delicate hankie was soaked.

He stood, crouched to a half-bent position and made his way to the empty chair next to Lily. Lily glanced at him; a look of surprise mixed with embarrassment touched her face. A new flood of tears burst the dam. Without a word, he reached into his pocket and withdrew a clean, white handkerchief and handed it to her.

Sniffing, she accepted the gift and promptly blew her nose. The noise drew the attention of nearby guests. Heads turned in their direction. Eric glared at those staring. Quickly they turned away.

He leaned close, catching a familiar whiff of wildflowers. "Are you a friend of the bride?" he whispered in her ear.

She shook her head.

"Friend of the groom?"

Again she shook her head.

"Then why are you crying?"

"I can't help it," she said in a tear-filled voice. "I always cry at weddings."

He laughed out loud. Heads turned again. He forced himself to be quiet. "Lily, Lily, Lily, what am I going to do with you? You're a hopeless romantic."

Her chin quivered as she jutted it out. "Don't make fun of me, Eric."

"Never."

His amusement faded, only to be replaced with an unexpected bout of tenderness. He draped an arm around her shoulder, squeezing it gently. In a heartbeat, he realized how right it felt to be there, touching her, comforting her.

Lily Gerard was like no woman he'd ever met.

They were as opposite as two people could possibly be. She was an optimist with a heart of pure gold. He was a skeptic, always waiting for the other shoe to drop. He looked at this wedding and saw a nightmare in the making. She saw a fairy tale.

She was a breath of fresh air in a stuffy, predictable world.

His hand stilled on her shoulder. With the force of a lightning bolt striking on a clear and sunny day, the realization hit him, taking his breath away. He'd finally figured out why he couldn't look Lily in the eye without a lump of guilt lodging in his throat.

Lily deserved the fairy tale.

She deserved the happily-ever-after ending.

She deserved a husband to go along with the child she was carrying.

Chapter Five

Eric's grip on her shoulder tightened. Through a veil of tears, Lily studied him. He was staring straight ahead at the bride and groom, his eyes wide, unblinking. His dark features had taken on a pale cast. He appeared positively green around the edges.

"Something wrong, Eric? You look sick."

"I must be, if I think what I think I'm thinking," he muttered.

She narrowed her eyes. "You want to run that by me again?"

"Never mind." He gave his head a slow, disbelieving shake. "I've got to get out of here. Get some fresh air. The walls are starting to close in on me." He rose from his chair, then stopped, frowning. "Are you free for dinner tonight?"

She nodded. "But are you sure—"

"I'm fine, just feeling a little claustrophobic. I'll pick you up at seven."

"Seven," she repeated, watching as he half walked, half ran from the living room.

If Eric was claustrophobic about anything, it was weddings. Usually he avoided the gatherings like a bad case of the hives. She glanced at the bride and groom kissing at the front of the room and smiled. All this love and happiness must have been too much for the cynical side of Eric. Poor boy, it'll probably take him hours to recover.

Hours later, Eric didn't seem much better. Dressed casually in white pants and dark polo shirt, he looked the part of a man about to have dinner with an old friend. But he acted as skittish as a tumbleweed dancing across the desert floor.

The Mexican restaurant he suggested for dinner was a favorite of theirs, a place they'd frequented often. Lily took his choice as a good sign. She hoped this meant Eric was ready for their relationship to return to normal. The way it was before she'd become pregnant.

Dimly lit, with rough stone floors and primitive wood chairs and tables, the restaurant exuded an Old World romance. Lily sipped a glass of water as she lingered over her menu. The dishes were all so good she always had a hard time deciding what to order.

Eric, on the other hand, opened his menu, gave it a cursory glance, then snapped it shut. She glanced at him as he sat impatiently drumming his fingers on the tabletop.

Lily closed her menu. As though on cue, a slender, dark-haired waitress came to take their orders. Eric ordered a taco salad. Lily's bouts with queasiness were becoming less frequent. When they did crop up, they occurred in the mornings. By evening she was starving.

She ordered a sampler platter of chimichangas, tacos, enchiladas and refried beans.

Eric eyed her skeptically after the waitress left. "That's a lot of food. I take it you aren't sick anymore?"

She dug a tortilla chip into a bowl of salsa. "I told you at the wedding—I'm feeling much better. In fact, lately I've been hungry all the time."

"Uh-huh."

The closest thing she'd seen to a smile since the evening began teased his lips.

"Next thing you know you'll be gaining weight, too."

Her chin jutted out. "Is that supposed to be a hint?"

"Not at all."

He blessed her with a full, easy smile, melting any lingering doubts she may have had. She had a feeling this evening was going to be special.

"This may sound like a cliché, but pregnancy agrees with you, Lily. You look great."

"Thank you," she said, blushing at the unexpected compliment.

As quickly as it had formed, Eric's smile faded. Once again, he returned to the nervous habit of drumming his fingers on the table.

"Eric, what's wrong?" she asked, sighing. "You've been acting so odd since the wedding this afternoon."

"Nothing's wrong, I just . . ." He muttered an oath. "I was going to wait until after dinner to ask you, but I guess now is as good a time as any."

"Ask me what?"

"Actually it's more of a proposition."

She frowned. "What sort of proposition?"

"Don't worry, Lily. It's strictly business." He reached into the breast pocket of his shirt and withdrew a yellow sheet of paper, unfolding it as he spoke. "I'll be honest,

Lily. I've been trying not to let it bother me. But dealing with your pregnancy has left me feeling a little uncomfortable."

"So that's what all this nervousness has been about," she said, collapsing against the back of her chair. "I wondered how long it would take before the old Eric Mitchell would resurface."

"Excuse me?"

"This idea of yours...wanting to help me with my pregnancy. You've finally realized you aren't cut out for the job." She smiled at the stunned look on his face. "Don't worry, Eric. I'm not angry. In fact, I'm relieved."

The expression on his face—surprise, now mixed with anger?—stopped her.

"You're relieved that I'm trying to back out of my promise to help you with your pregnancy?"

Her smile faded. "I don't blame you, Eric. You can't push yourself into being something you just aren't."

"And what would that be?"

Lily shifted in her chair. "Let's just say it's been a bit out of character for you to be so attentive, so responsible." The words tumbled out in a rush. "Not that I've minded. It's been nice having someone to fuss over me. But now it's time for things to get back to normal."

"Normal?"

"Well, maybe not normal. I mean, I am still pregnant. And if something comes up I'd like to be able to count on your help. But I don't want you to feel obligated to check up on me so often. I'm sure you have better things to do with your time." She swallowed hard. "Like dating again."

He raised a brow. "You want me to see other women?"

She leaned closer, her tone confiding. "Eric, when I asked you to be a sperm donor, you had to give up a few—" she cleared her throat "—recreational activities. Now that I'm pregnant, you don't have to do without..." She paused and glanced around the restaurant, making sure she wouldn't be overheard. "Eric, you don't have to be celibate any longer."

A spark of amusement glinted in his eyes. "What makes you think I'm not already partaking in a few *recreational activities?*"

Her eyes widened. "Are you?"

She regretted the question as soon as she'd asked it. Early in their relationship, they'd made it an unspoken policy not to discuss each other's love life. Not that she had a love life to discuss. But she knew Eric saw other women. Lots of other women.

For some reason, discussing Eric's personal life had always made her uncomfortable. So she never asked for details. Which suited Eric just fine, since he seemed reluctant to share that part of his life with her, also. Nothing had changed this, she told herself sternly. Just because Eric had fathered her child, it didn't mean he suddenly had to give her an accounting of his comings and goings.

To her growing dismay, Eric didn't appear offended by her question. Instead he looked pleased.

"No, Lily. I'm not seeing anyone at the moment."

His answer left her feeling oddly relieved. A flush of embarrassing heat blossomed on her face. She dropped her eyes to her clenched fingers, unable to face him. "You should, you know. It's time for you to stop putting your life on hold. You've done more than enough for me already."

"I don't agree," he said, his tone sincere.

Her eyes met his. His expression was somber.

"No matter what I do, it just doesn't seem to be enough. I can't shake the feeling that I should be doing more to help you...and the baby."

"Eric—"

"When I saw you at the wedding, I realized that what I've been feeling is a case of delayed guilt."

Guilt? Her heart thumped a warning beat against her chest. She started to protest.

He raised a hand, stopping her. "This isn't easy for me, Lily. Just hear me out. You've always been so traditional about marriage and family that the way you became pregnant has bothered me."

"Eric, there's nothing for you to feel guilty about." She enunciated each and every word with care. She wanted to be sure he understood her message. "I'm very happy with the way I became pregnant."

"Well, I'm not. I saw your reaction at the wedding today." He shook his head. "All those tears over a marriage that'll probably last six months. Anyone with that much blind faith in marriage vows should be having a baby as a married woman. Not single and alone."

Lily stared at him. Eric sounded so provincial, so unlike himself.

"Have you considered the repercussions your pregnancy may cause you?" he asked.

"Don't be ridiculous, Eric. In this day and age, being a single mother isn't a stigma. No one cares."

"Is that so?" He leaned back in his chair, giving her an assessing glance. "What do you think your clients are going to say when they find out the woman selling them wedding cakes is pregnant and refuses to marry?"

She opened her mouth, then snapped it shut, realizing she didn't have a ready answer. There was a possibility that some clients might disapprove when they learned of her choice to become a single mother. But it was a risk she'd have to deal with when the time came.

"You sell more than wedding cakes, Lily." His voice gentled. "You sell fairy tales. You believe in romance and happy endings. I know this from experience because you've tried to sell me on the idea of marriage too many times to count. If you weren't so stubborn, you'd admit you'd rather have this baby the usual way. You'd rather be married."

"I don't have to admit anything, Eric. This entire conversation is pointless. I'm already pregnant. It's too late to change my mind now."

"It's not too late." He paused, taking a deep breath. "I'm willing to marry you, Lily."

"M-marry me?"

The *M* word. Alarm bells sounded in her mind. The hairs lifted on the back of her neck. The last man to propose to her was dead. Eric's proposal felt like a harbinger of misfortune.

Oblivious to her growing distress, Eric continued, "Of course our relationship doesn't have to change. Our marriage would be strictly business. I've written down a sketchy proposal for you to take a look at." He handed her the sheet of yellow, legal-size paper.

Curiosity kept her from grabbing the paper out of his hands and ripping it into tiny shreds. Stiffly she accepted the sheet.

"Basically, all it says is that your property remains yours and what is mine stays mine. Of course, once you've had the baby and the marriage is dissolved, you'll have full parental custody. But I'm willing to give you a reasonable amount of child support if you decide you need it."

His impersonal, businesslike tone snapped her out of her trance. Eric knew how strongly she felt about love and marriage. And yet he'd had the nerve to propose a marriage of convenience. She'd warned him about the curse, her family's bad luck with marriages. In fact, he was the only person she'd ever trusted enough to confide her guilty secret. But he'd chosen to ignore her warning. A slow flame of anger took the place of fear.

Lily dropped the paper as though her fingers had been burned. She sat back in her chair, closed her eyes and counted to ten to steady her rising anger. She felt the weight of Eric's concerned gaze as he watched her. Her eyes snapped open. Counting had done nothing to cool her temper.

She stood. Grasping the edge of the table with both hands, she leaned toward Eric. "I'm leaving. Now."

Not bothering to see whether he followed, she turned and left. On her way out the door, she stopped at the hostess desk and asked her to call a taxi.

She stepped outside into the night. She shivered despite the warm desert air that bathed her skin. Eric had pushed aside her fears and beliefs in order to soothe his own guilty conscience. The realization left her feeling cold and empty inside.

She felt betrayed.

Eric tossed a handful of money onto the table and hurried to catch Lily. He found her in the center of the courtyard, studying the water falling from a Spanish-style fountain in a small wishing pool. Her back was stiff. One foot tapped a steady beat on the rugged cobblestone floor. Her hands were planted firmly on her slender hips. It didn't take a genius to figure out he'd made her angry. Very angry.

Good, he told himself, that made two of them.

Didn't she realize how difficult proposing marriage had been for him? Her blunt rejection had dredged up all the unpleasant memories of his last, failed attempt at marriage. But for some unexplainable reason, Lily's refusal felt worse.

Much worse.

More than his pride had been wounded by Lily's rejection. Something else, something much more painful, had been involved. He cared for Lily. He truly thought his offer would please her. She'd done more than reject his marriage proposal. She'd rejected him.

He took a deep breath, forcing himself to remain calm. She didn't acknowledge his presence even as he stood next to her.

"Let's try to be reasonable about this," he began, struggling to keep his voice even.

Lily swung around to glare at him. "Reasonable? You want me to be reasonable?"

He took a step back. "What are you getting so upset about? I just asked you to marry me?"

"Let me tell you something, Eric Mitchell. I'm not in the market for a husband. Not now. Not ever. So you can just forget about your proposition." She pointed an accusing finger at him. "And even if I were looking for a husband, I wouldn't accept a proposal as cold and heartless as yours."

Eric felt stunned, as though he'd been slapped by the unfairness of her accusation. Heartless? Hadn't he offered child support? He thought he'd gone out of his way to be fair and considerate.

His jaw stiffened. "What's the matter with my proposal?"

"Property settlement, marriage dissolution, child custody..." She jabbed her finger at his chest as she ticked off each of his offenses. "How could you mention the word *contract* in the same breath as something as beautiful as a marriage proposal?"

He threw his hands up in the air in a gesture of defeat. "Forget I asked. I was just trying to do you a favor."

"A favor?" A shiver ran down his back as she said the words slowly. "How dare you call that... that proposition a favor?"

Eric prided himself on the fact that under most circumstances he could keep a cool, even demeanor. A real boon for someone whose patience was tried on a regular basis in a courtroom setting. But Lily had pushed him to his limit. He felt an anger sweep over him as hot and quick as a brush fire over dry kindling.

"I don't get it," he said, his voice edged with his growing anger. "We're friends, Lily, not lovers. My marriage proposal, albeit more business than personal, shouldn't have offended you. There has to be some other reason you're so mad."

She took a moment before answering. When she did speak, her voice broke. It was then he realized pain had replaced her anger.

"How could you have forgotten about the curse, Eric? Your marriage proposal proves you never believed a word I said."

A lump of guilt stuck in his throat. The last thing he'd intended was to hurt Lily. But she was right. He *had* forgotten about her curse because he *didn't* believe it. Flames of frustration licked his anger. "That's what this is all about? Your damned curse?"

"You don't have to shout, Eric. I'm the one who's the injured party here, not you."

"Don't start spouting legal jargon at me, Lily Gerard. I'm the lawyer, remember?"

"Then start acting like one," she hollered. "You've lost this case, counselor. Admit your defeat with grace."

"Not when it comes to something so ridiculous. I'll never—do you hear me, Lily?—never accept your curse."

She raised her chin defiantly. "And I'll never accept your marriage proposal."

A flag of challenge had just been waved in front of him. No one, not even Lily Gerard and ten curses, could stop him from getting his way.

"You know what I think, Lily?" he asked, his tone low, confiding. He took a step closer. "I think you're scared."

Her eyes widened defensively. "I am not."

"Yes, you are. You're scared to admit I'm right. That you'd rather be married."

"To someone like you?" She smiled, looking amused. "Not hardly."

He ignored the insult. "There's no risk, no pain when you don't allow yourself to feel anything at all. You're safe when you hide behind that curse of yours, aren't you?"

Her smile faded. Her green eyes glinted like beautiful, icy emeralds. "How dare you badger me, when I've thought of nothing but your safety?"

"My safety?" Chuckling, he took another step toward her, closing the distance between them. He touched a finger to the curve of her mouth. "Tell me, Lily. Do these lips really carry the kiss of death?"

Her lips trembled. He felt her sharp intake of air against his finger, knowing he'd overstepped the limit of her strained patience. Lily's temper was about to explode. Angry or not, he just couldn't seem to stop himself.

She tossed her head back, forcing him to drop his hand.

"Whether or not my lips are fatal is something you'll never know."

He'd always been a fool for a challenge.

"Never say never, Lily," he growled. Before she could move away, he cupped the back of her neck with one hand, her waist with the other and drew her toward him.

A shock wave of pleasure ricocheted through him as their lips met. Warm and lush, her mouth felt as though it had been molded just to be kissed by him. He hesitated, then deepened the kiss. He teased her lips with his tongue, tasting the spicy flavor of salsa and a sweetness that could only be Lily.

She slid her hands between Eric and her, resting them on his shoulders.

He expected her to push him away.

She didn't.

Instead she wrapped her arms around his neck, bringing them closer. He breathed in sharply as her supple curves met and shaped the hard contours of his body. The scent of wildflowers filled the air. Her breasts, soft and full, pressed against his chest. Her stomach nuzzled his hips. He felt his body harden in response.

The kiss was started as a challenge, an act of pure defiance. But stronger, more basic emotions took its place. Desire raced through him, overriding his common sense. Even more disturbing, in Lily's arms he felt a contentment so deep, so fulfilling he never wanted it to end. He felt as though he'd finally come home after a long and painful absence.

He groaned inwardly, fighting for restraint. Then her lips parted. Her tongue met his, silently encouraging him to deepen the kiss. He gave in to desire, crushing her against him.

A breathy sound escaped her lips as she surrendered fully to the demands of his kiss. Like the voice of reason, the sound whispered in his ear, cooling his passion-heated body, bringing him slowly to his senses.

Kissing Lily had been unplanned. Enjoying it had been unexpected. But what he felt now went beyond mere enjoyment. His body thrummed with a lusty need.

Lily was his best friend. He cared more about her than any woman he'd ever known. Caring and lusting were a dangerous combination. Together they could make a man do stupid things—like giving his heart to a woman who obviously wasn't interested in catching it.

An unfamiliar sense of panic rose in his chest. For the first time in his life, Eric felt as though he'd lost control.

Somehow, Lily had lost control.

Feelings that had been carefully suppressed for more than three years came awake with a lightning bolt of awareness. Blood pulsed hot and rapid through her veins. Her body sizzled wherever Eric touched her. The icy chill that had kept a lock on her heart since David's death vaporized in a haze of sensuous heat.

Confusion and disappointment broke through the haze as she felt Eric pull back and abruptly end the kiss. He stepped away, his back to the pool, and stared at her with a glazed, shocked look in his eyes.

The fog lifted. Lily stared at him with an equal amount of disbelief. She'd just kissed her best friend. She didn't know whether she wanted to smack him or kiss him again.

She gave a silent moan. She wanted to kiss him.

"What did you do that for?" she demanded, trying not to think about her own wanton behavior.

"Me?" He shot her an incredulous glance. "You weren't exactly fighting me off, Lily."

Embarrassed, she pressed her palms to her face. Her skin felt flushed. Her body tingled with a fluid heat. Her pulse was racing. For the first time in years, she felt alive. Fully, passionately alive.

And Eric, the father of her unborn child, had made her feel this way. The realization hit her hard, like an unexpected dunking with an icy-cold bucket of water. A bitter taste filled her mouth. She felt as though she were going to be sick.

Eric, on the other hand, seemed to have recovered from his shock—almost.

He took a step back, a strained smile on his lips. "Nothing happened, Lily." He raised his hands, palms flat and facing the heavens. "The sky didn't crash down upon my head. The earth didn't swallow me up." His attempt at humor seemed forced. He back-stepped again. "Nothing happened."

She plastered a smile on her face, hiding her growing irritation. If nothing had happened, why did he keep moving away from her?

Eric's next step was his last.

Her smile dissolved. She gasped as his leg hit the edge of the pool and tipped him off-balance. She reached a hand out for him, but it was too late.

Eric fell backward into the pool.

She watched in horror as he sputtered and splashed in the shallow water. He struggled to his feet. He stood in knee-deep water, drenched from head to toe.

Once she saw that he was all right, a bubble of laughter rose in her throat. "Serves you right, Eric."

"This isn't funny, Lily. I could have killed myself." He scowled, tossing his head back and sending a ribbon of water over his shoulder. "Forget I said that."

The laughter died on her lips. Once again reminded of the curse, she felt her spirits sink. "I tried to warn you." Her smile was bittersweet. "Looks as though I've won this round, counselor."

A horn honked. Her taxi had arrived. With a saucy swing of her hips, she turned and strode away.

"Where do you think you're going?" Eric was stunned. "Come back here, Lily. This isn't finished."

Keeping her back to him, she lifted a hand and waved goodbye as she got into the taxi. When Eric was no longer in her sight, her bravado disappeared. Her heart fell like a rock. Alone in the shadows of the taxi's back seat, she gave in to the tears that threatened.

"Where to, lady?" the driver asked.

She choked back the tears long enough to give him her address. She wrapped her arm around her waist and tried to stop the tremors that shook her. She pressed her quivering lips together and felt the lingering touch of Eric's kiss.

She'd never forgive Eric.

He'd given her a taste for something that could never be hers. He'd made her want again. He'd made her feel again.

Eric fumed with anger as he watched Lily escape. He'd kissed her to prove a point—that her curse was nonsense. But the only thing he'd proved was his own stupidity. How was he supposed to know that he'd enjoy the kiss so much?

A couple leaving the restaurant eyed him curiously. With a flush of embarrassment, he realized he was still standing in the pool. Waves lapped against the concrete walls as he waded to the side of the pool and stepped out.

Water streamed off his body, plastering his clothes to his skin. He walked to his car, leaving a trail behind him.

Serves you right, Eric. Her words followed him. He gritted his teeth. He needed a dip in the pool to cool his overactive libido. But did Lily always have to be right?

Eric jerked open the door of his Porsche. He glanced down at his wet clothes, then at the leather seats. He shook his head. His poor car would never be the same. Cringing, he plopped his wet body into the driver's seat. He inserted the key into the ignition, but didn't start the engine. He couldn't stop thinking about Lily.

Her lips were dangerous, but certainly not lethal. He smiled, recalling their kiss. His body reacted to the memory, making the fit of his water-soaked pants even more uncomfortable. Who'd have thought a pint-size redhead could wallop such a punch? He wondered what it would have been like to tempt fate and make a baby with Lily the old-fashioned way.

Not that he had a snowball's chance in hell of finding out. He scowled, recalling her blunt rejection of his proposal. He ground the key in the ignition and threw the shift into reverse. His tires squealed as he drove his car through the lot.

Self-righteous indignation snaked its way through his mind, rekindling a path of hot anger. He'd tried to do the right thing. He'd proposed. She'd turned him down. If he were smart, he'd accept her refusal.

Nobody had ever said he was smart when it came to understanding women.

Kissing Lily had given him a taste of the forbidden fruit. If he accepted her refusal, he might lose more than a chance at paradise. He might lose his best friend. Unease tightened his chest. Life without Lily seemed like a bleak prospect.

He tromped his foot down on the accelerator. All Lily needed was a little persuasion to see that marrying him was the right thing to do. He'd admit his initial approach may have been a bit cold. He'd have to warm her up to the idea. Fresh encouragement surged through his veins. He knew just the way to win her over.

Lily had a weakness for romance. She'd made him watch *Casablanca* at least ten times in the past three years. Her favorite book was *Gone With The Wind*. A niggling of doubt sought and found a foothold in his upbeat mood. He tried not to be discouraged by the fact that the heroines in both had met with unhappy endings.

Eric sighed. Lily was the most stubborn romantic he knew. She sold romance in the guise of wedding cakes every single day. She'd accused him of being unromantic. He would prove her wrong. Romance would be his most powerful weapon.

A flashing red light in the rearview mirror caught his eye. He groaned, his uplifted spirits plummeting. He eased up on the accelerator and pulled his car over to the side of the road. Since he'd asked Lily to marry him, bad luck seemed to be dogging him. If he were a superstitious man, he would take all of this as an omen. He watched the police officer's approach in his mirror.

Good thing he wasn't a superstitious man.

Chapter Six

"Mrs. Spencer, you and your ex-husband were given joint custody of Bridget," Eric explained to the woman on the other end of the phone line. "You'll be going against a court order if you refuse him his visitation rights."

Mrs. Hunter entered his office carrying a long white florist's box. Eric motioned for her to bring it to his desk.

"She isn't eating."

He whisked the tag off the box. In a bold slash, Lily's name had been deleted from the tag. In its place she'd written, "Return to sender."

Eric sighed. "And she wakes up at night howling?"

Some of his cases were more unusual than others. *Spencer v. Spencer* had to be one of his most memorable. Bridget, a toy poodle, had been like a child to the Spencers. When they'd divorced, both Mr. and Mrs. Spencer had insisted on full custody of the dog. The judge had decided in favor of joint custody, a ruling his client did not like.

"Mrs. Spencer, I'm not an expert, but I do admit it sounds as though Bridget is troubled. Why don't you make an appointment with her veterinarian so that we can rule out any physical reason for her behavior? Once that's been taken care of, we'll go from there."

He said his goodbyes and hung up the phone.

"Still trying to nail her ex on cruelty charges?" Mrs. Hunter asked, not bothering to hide an amused smile.

Eric nodded. "You've got to hand it to her—she is persistent."

"Persistent?" Mrs. Hunter scoffed. "Try stubborn. The woman doesn't know when to quit." She tapped a finger on the box of flowers. "Speaking of knowing when to quit..."

Eric scowled.

"How many boxes of flowers have you and Lily exchanged this week—two?"

"Three," he said, deciding it best not to mention the candy or the returned cards. He stood, picked up the flowers and handed them to his secretary. "Here, they're all yours."

"Thanks, boss. But I do hope you bought something other than roses this time. My office is beginning to smell like a funeral home."

Eric didn't smile. He found nothing amusing about the situation. His plan to win Lily's forgiveness had fallen flat on its romantic nose.

Mrs. Hunter eyed him curiously. "Why don't you try a more direct approach? Like talking to her?"

He dug his hands into his pants pockets. "She's not taking my calls. I've gone to the bakery, but she isn't in. When I go to her house, her car's parked out front, but she won't answer the door."

"I may be butting in where I don't belong but I can't help myself. I have to know. What in the world did you do to that girl to make her so mad?"

Eric hesitated, embarrassed to admit to his secretary the real reason for Lily's temper. He shrugged, trying to appear nonchalant. "I offered to marry her."

Mrs. Hunter dropped herself into the chair opposite his desk, a stunned expression on her face. "I don't believe it. *You* asked Lily to marry you?"

"Not exactly asked. It was more like...an arrangement."

She quirked an eyebrow. "What sort of an arrangement?"

"A business arrangement."

"Oh, Eric," Mrs. Hunter said disgustedly. "No wonder she's mad at you."

He put his hands up in mock surrender. "I already know I made a mistake. But how can I apologize if she won't take my calls?"

"Well, it's obvious something as lame as flowers isn't going to work," she said, giving the box a pat. She narrowed a gaze at him. "You still want to marry her?"

He hedged a direct answer. "I asked, didn't I?"

At the moment, having Lily return his calls seemed more urgent. His unease at the thought of losing her friendship had grown to panic. Life without her left him feeling hollow inside. He missed his best friend. He missed Lily.

"I never thought I'd see the day. Well, you can't ask a woman to marry you—the right way—if she won't talk to you. Lily's as stubborn as you are. Worse, in fact."

"Thanks a lot," he said, shooting her an indignant look.

"What we have to do is not give her a choice." Thoughtfully she rubbed her cheek. "A woman loves it when a man makes a fool of himself over her."

Eric grimaced, recalling his unplanned swim in the restaurant's pool. As far as he was concerned, he'd made a big enough fool of himself already.

Mrs. Hunter snapped her fingers, smiling with manic glee. "I've got the perfect idea."

Eric's chest tightened. He recognized the look on his secretary's face. It meant trouble with a capital *T*. Whatever the idea was, he already hated it.

"Lily, someone's out front asking for you."

Lily glanced up at Ann, who was standing in the doorway of her office. She tossed her pen on the desk and slammed the scheduling book closed with a thud. "If it's Eric, I'm not here."

Ann smiled. "It isn't Eric."

"Who is it?"

"I think you'd better come see for yourself," she said, her answer as mysterious as the expression on her face.

"Ann, I hate surprises. Tell me what's going on," she moaned.

"Come on, Lily. Where's your spirit of adventure?" Ann took her arm and pulled her through the deserted kitchen.

"Where is everyone?" she asked, her stomach churning with trepidation.

"Out front," Ann said, pushing her through the doorway leading to the showroom.

Lily skidded to a stop when she saw what awaited her.

A *mariachi band,* complete with Spanish guitars and brass horns, was assembled in the center of her showroom. Her staff had formed a semicircle around the group, looking anxious for the show to begin.

The leader of the band, wearing a heavily decorated jacket and a large sombrero and carrying a guitar, approached her. "Mrs. Gerard?" he asked, a smile twitching beneath his thick, dark mustache.

She nodded, too shocked to speak.

"We are a mariachi band, roaming minstrels of love. Mr. Mitchell has asked us to play for you a ballad about a young man whose heart is broken. In this song the young man asks for his lover's forgiveness."

She felt the eyes of her staff watching her. A blush crept slowly across her face.

The leader motioned for his band to start. Music, loud, beautiful music, meant for an open courtyard or a ball-room-size room, filled the bakery. The windows shook. The display cabinets danced. The small showroom vibrated with the pulsing beat.

Her staff smiled, enjoying themselves immensely.

Lily wished the ground would open up and swallow her whole. Embarrassment flooded her entire body. This time Eric had gone too far.

Soon the song ended. Lily hurried to the cash register and drew out a handful of money. "Thank you so much," she said, trying to pay the leader. "The song was beautiful."

With a sweep of his hand, he waved the bribe away. "Our next song is about star-crossed lovers."

The music began again.

Lily leaned an elbow on the counter and slumped against a display cabinet. This was her own fault, she told herself, glancing around the showroom at her staff. She'd involved them in her battle to avoid Eric. She'd asked them to lie whenever he called, telling him she wasn't in.

They saw her returning his flowers, unopened. It was only fitting that they witness her humiliation now.

The song ended. Once again she offered the leader her money.

He smiled. "You don't understand, Mrs. Gerard. Mr. Mitchell is the only one who can ask us to stop."

"Excuse me?"

"We've been instructed to play for you until we are told by Mr. Mitchell to stop."

Lily glanced out the bakery windows, expecting to see Eric standing in the courtyard. A few curious passersby had their noses pressed to the window as they watched the show with interest, but there was no sign of Eric.

She raised her hands palms upward in a helpless gesture. "But how . . . ?"

He nodded toward the phone resting on the counter. "A phone call will do."

He strode back to the band. The music started . . . again.

Lily closed her eyes and began to count. She got to three before her head began to throb along with the beat of the music. Muttering an unladylike expletive, Lily stomped over to the phone and punched in Eric's number.

His secretary answered on the second ring. Lily swore she heard Mrs. Hunter chuckling before she transferred her call to Eric.

"Lily, what a surprise."

She could barely hear him over the blare of the music. "Call off your band, Eric."

"What did you say, Lily? I couldn't quite hear you."

"Your band, Eric," she shouted. "Call them off."

The staff turned curious gazes toward her. She ducked her head in embarrassment.

"Not until you agree to talk to me."

"I *am* talking to you."

"Uh-uh, face-to-face."

She sighed. "All right. I'll talk to you."

"When?"

"Tonight, after work."

"Where?"

She chewed on her lower lip, recalling his kiss with alarming clarity. Somewhere neutral and, preferably, public would be best for their meeting. "A restaurant?"

"Nope, we tried that already. Remember? When you dumped me in the pool."

Her body went rigid. "I did not—"

"My place, seven o'clock."

Countless women had lost their wits and virtue at Eric's home in Paradise Valley. That was the last place she wanted to meet him. "No. My house, seven-thirty."

"I'll be there."

"Now, about the band," she said, her voice pleading.

"Let me talk to Mr. Ramirez."

Lily could almost hear the triumphant smile in Eric's voice. She handed the phone to the leader. She ground her teeth, fighting her rising irritation as she watched Mr. Ramirez nod obsequiously.

Ramirez smiled broadly when he hung up the phone. With a snap of his fingers, the band stopped. He waved away the money Lily handed him. "Mr. Mitchell has already taken care of payment for our services."

She forced a smile. "Then thank you for your beautiful music, Mr. Ramirez."

"No thanks are necessary. I am pleased to have been instrumental in patching up a lovers' spat between you and Mr. Mitchell."

Aware of her staff watching her, a captive audience in this show of shows, Lily didn't bother to argue. She pressed her fingertips to her forehead and shook her head in defeat. Mr. Ramirez and his band left. Lily strode back to her office, slamming the door behind her.

Thanks to Eric and her own petulant behavior, her staff thought she and Eric were lovers. Once her pregnancy was known, their assumptions would be confirmed. How could she have let things get so out of hand? How was she going to live through the next eight months?

She collapsed into her office chair. The next eight months? She had more pressing matters to worry about. She had tonight with Eric to live through.

"What? No flowers?"

Eric grinned. "Sorry, three dozen roses in one week is my limit."

Despite her nervous misgivings, Lily couldn't help but smile. "Roses, eh? I wondered what they were."

"You could have opened them and found out for yourself."

She raised her chin. "I wasn't *that* interested.'

"So I noticed." He raised a brow, looking curious. "Why didn't you return the chocolates?"

She shrugged. "A moment of weakness. I was hungry. The mariachi band was a nice touch, though. Very *you*, Eric. Loud and hard to ignore."

His smile deepened. "It worked, didn't it?"

They lapsed into an awkward silence, standing in the doorway of her house, assessing each other with wary gazes. Eric's dark hair and tanned skin contrasted with his white polo shirt, reminding her of chocolate icing against white cake.

Her mouth watered.

He wore a pair of faded jeans, which molded to the muscles of his legs. And he had on Docksiders without socks. Eric looked handsome, sexy . . . delicious.

"May I come in? Or do we have to talk on your doorstep?" His voice carried a hint of its usual humor.

Lily felt her body relax. She stepped back, motioning for him to enter. "Come in."

The air stirred as he passed. The scent of his citrus-and-spice after-shave filled her nostrils. Her stomach growled with renewed hunger. Tonight everything about Eric reminded her of food.

"Where would you like to talk?" she asked, keeping her tone casual. "Outside? By the pool?"

"No thanks. I'd like to stay as far away from water as possible."

Lily bit back a smile. "Then why don't we have a seat in the living room?"

"Fine by me," Eric said, moving from the foyer into the living room.

She followed him. Eric took a seat on the blue-and-white striped sofa, his large frame dwarfing the delicate lines of the furniture. He left plenty of room for her to sit next to him, but Lily avoided the temptation and chose the matching blue club chair on the opposite side of the room.

Eric draped an arm across the back of the sofa and studied her with a wordless intensity. Lily crossed her legs and tugged at the hem of her white shorts, wishing she'd worn pants, which would have shown a little less skin.

"Are you ever going to stop being mad at me, Lily?"

His question took her by surprise. She stared at him, not sure how to answer.

"I want to make things right between us. I miss my best friend." His brown-eyed gaze looked sincere. "I've missed you, Lily."

She felt her resistance ebb. She'd missed him, too. She missed the unexpected, but welcome, phone calls they made to each other. The casual conversations they shared over dinner. His caring embrace when the day seemed dim and she needed a hug to cheer her up. She missed them all. But she didn't know how they could ever get back what had been lost between them.

"I miss you, too, Eric. But things can never be the same between us."

"Don't say that."

She dropped her gaze to her fisted hands. "Our friendship changed when you asked me to marry you."

"No."

The single word reverberated in the room. She raised her eyes. Their gazed locked and held.

"Our friendship changed when you asked me to father your child."

Her back stiffened. "I only wanted your sperm, Eric. Not a marriage proposal."

A vein at his temple pulsed rapidly, the only sign Eric was irritated. "That's right, Lily. My sperm. No one else's, but mine."

"What are you saying? That I've been carrying around some hidden attraction toward you all these years?" She scowled. "Look, Eric, if this has something to do with that kiss—"

"That kiss . . . was nice, but unexpected. It has nothing to do with the point I'm making. You asked me to be a sperm donor because you needed my help. Whether you want to admit it or not, you're afraid of going through this pregnancy alone."

Lily opened her mouth to protest.

Eric didn't give her the chance. He continued, "You knew I wouldn't let you fend for yourself, because we're friends. I asked you to marry me to take that friendship one step further." He shrugged nonchalantly. "As I see it, the fact that we enjoyed kissing each other is merely icing on the cake.''

Did he have to mention food?

Lily jumped to her feet and moved to the fireplace. She stared at the empty hearth, trying to steady her shaking limbs.

Icing on the cake. Being considered a reward for good behavior didn't sit well. But Eric was right about one thing: the thought of going through nine months of pregnancy alone had scared her. Knowing he'd be there to allay her fears had made her decision to have a baby that much easier.

She sighed. Eric's refusal to take the blame for the breach in their friendship surprised her. She'd expected him to dance around their argument, coaxing her out of her anger with his wit and humor. She hadn't expected him to be so blunt, so honest.

She felt the heavy measure of his gaze. Slowly she turned to face him. He remained quiet, forcing her to be the first to speak.

''I'll agree,'' she said finally. ''We're both to blame for things getting out of hand. But that doesn't change the way we feel. We can't go back to being friends just because we want it to happen.''

''You're right. We'll have to work at it.''

With all her heart, she wanted to believe him. She needed to believe him. But a stubborn thread of disbelief wound its way through her mind.

''I don't know.'' She shook her head. ''So much has happened.''

''It'll never work if you're too afraid to try.''

She straightened her shoulders. ''I'm not afraid.''

"Of course you're not." He chuckled. "And you haven't been looking at me as though I were the big bad wolf about to gobble you up, either."

"I have not," she said indignantly.

"Oh?" He raised a brow. "Then why are you standing all the way across the room? I have to shout to make myself heard."

"You're being ridiculous."

"Prove it." He patted the sofa cushion. "Come here, Lily. Show me you're not afraid."

She hesitated only a moment before she crossed the room to join him on the sofa. Her bare leg brushed against the soft, worn material of his jeans as she sat down next to him. He kept his arm draped across the back of the sofa. She felt its gentle weight pressed against her shoulders. Fluid heat warmed her body. She remembered their kiss. She remembered the feel of his strong, hard body against hers. She gave a silent moan. Sitting this close to Eric was a mistake.

"That's not so bad, is it?" he asked.

She shook her head, not trusting herself to speak.

"So, what do we do next?"

"Forget the past four weeks ever happened," she suggested.

He shifted against the cushions. She shivered as the tips of his fingers grazed her shoulder.

"I'm supposed to forget you're pregnant?"

"Well, no."

"Or maybe you'd rather we forgot my marriage proposal?"

She nodded. "That'd be a good place to start."

He sat back. His fingers traced the shoulder seam of her blouse, sending arrows of pleasure darting throughout her body.

"I bet you'd really like it if we forgot about the kiss."

"Eric—" She winced as her voice broke.

"I should try to forget how warm your lips were?" he asked, his voice a husky murmur.

Her pulse quickened. "Eric—"

"And how soft your body felt against mine?"

She told herself to move. But her body refused to cooperate.

"What about that sound you made when I kissed you? That breathy whisper that's been haunting me day and night."

She moaned, closing her eyes to blot out the image his words conjured up.

"Lily, did I ever tell you I have a perfect memory?" he asked, sounding sincere. "Darned thing's almost photographic. It's impossible for me to forget . . . anything."

The way he drawled out *anything* proved to be her undoing. She felt bewitched, as though she were being made love to with words, slowly and lazily. She opened her eyes to find him watching her, his gaze mirroring her own desire.

He pulled her into his arms. She went willingly.

Their lips met with a tender fierceness that thrilled and scared her all at once. She felt the impatient flick of his tongue. She opened her mouth, seeking the taste she'd been craving. The taste that was uniquely Eric.

Her hands moved with a restlessness of their own, twining themselves in the thick hair at the back of his head, then moving downward to explore the wide strength of his shoulders and back. His chest rose and fell beneath her fingers with each sharp intake of his breath.

With their mouths melded in a breathless embrace, she fell backward onto the cushions, bringing Eric along with her. He settled himself on the sofa next to her. Gasping for air, they broke apart. He gazed down upon her, his brown eyes shining, wanting.

"I lied," she said.

He frowned, looking puzzled.

"When I said we should forget. I don't think I ever want to forget the way you taste."

He smiled. "That makes two of us."

He dipped his head for another bite. His lips touched hers briefly. Then he covered her face with butterfly kisses, tracing her cheekbone, her jaw, her neck.

She felt him fumbling with the buttons of her blouse. One by one the buttons fell away, exposing more and more of her flesh. She shivered at the impact of cool air and his searing gaze against her skin.

Pregnancy, which made her breasts fuller, also made them more sensitive. He brushed the knuckles of his fingers against the lacy cup of her bra, teasing her. Her nipples hardened in response. She gasped when his mouth followed and he pressed his lips to the place where skin met lace.

"Eric," she murmured, closing her eyes and giving in to the shattering sensations that rocked her body.

She sensed him draw away. "I'm not hurting you, am I?"

Her lids felt heavy as she opened her eyes. Eric was studying her, his concern obvious.

"I've never—" He frowned, looking uncomfortable. "Making love to a pregnant woman is a first for me."

She smiled. "You're doing fine, Eric. Just fine." She tugged him down for another hungry kiss.

"Too bad we didn't realize this before we went to the fertility clinic," he whispered against her lips. "Making a baby the conventional way would have been a lot more interesting." He cupped his hands around her waist and brought her snug against him.

She sucked in a shaky breath, raking her fingernails over his back. "The time just wasn't right."

He lowered his mouth to nibble at the slope of her neck. "At least getting married will be a whole lot more fun."

"Getting married?" Her hand stilled on the small of his back. "We're not getting married."

"Of course we are."

"No, we're not."

Eric moaned. "Come on, Lily. Don't argue with me now."

She ignored the pained look on his face. "I *want* you, Eric. But I don't *want* to marry you."

"And what if I said I had too much respect for our friendship to make love to you any other way? What if I said, it's with the intention of marriage or not at all?"

Her eyes widened. "That'd be emotional blackmail."

He considered this for a moment. "You're right." His smile was playful. "It's a good thing I'm a man of principle. I couldn't live with myself if I'd blackmailed my best friend."

Repositioning himself so he was more comfortable, he continued his downward exploration, starting with the ticklish spot behind her ear.

Lily collapsed against the cushions, sighing, enjoying the sensations his lips were creating. However, in the back of her mind, the words *respect* and *friendship* kept resurfacing. She tried to shut them out, but like a guilty conscience, they wouldn't go away.

With a groan of frustration, she realized she couldn't go through with it. Eric was right. Their friendship was teetering in the balance. Making love to him might be the push needed to topple it over the edge.

"Wait." She sat up, almost knocking Eric off the sofa.

He grunted, grabbing her waist to catch himself before he hit the floor. "Now what?"

"Maybe we're being hasty."

He closed his eyes. A long-suffering expression crossed his face. "This had better be good."

"I think you're right. We're too good friends to have a casual affair."

His eyes flew open. He set his jaw in a stubborn line. "I've offered to marry you."

"And I've already said no. Eric, I don't want to lose our friendship. It's too important to me, especially now."

Sighing, he released her, allowing her to scramble to the opposite side of the sofa. Lily's hands felt clumsy as she straightened her clothes. Her body felt weak. She ached with an unfulfilled need.

"Let me get this straight," Eric said. "You won't make love to me without a commitment. I've asked you to marry me, but you've refused." He sighed tersely. "Does any of this make sense?"

Lily chewed on her lower lip. Her reasons had made more sense a minute ago. Now, faced with cold, lonely reality, she wasn't so sure.

"Let's hear it, Lily. Why won't you marry me?" he asked, tucking his shirttails into his jeans. He shot her a smoldering glance. "But I'm warning you, it better not be because of your damned curse."

Damned curse? A slow burn of irritation took arousal's place. "All right, Eric. Curses aside. You'd make a lousy husband."

He looked shocked. "What are you talking about?"

She searched her mind. "For one thing, you work too much."

"No more than I have to," he muttered.

She continued, "When you aren't working, you like to play. You'd never be able to settle into the dull routine of family life."

"That's not true."

"Of course it is. From the house you live in to the car you drive, everything about you is fast and expensive." She sighed, rising to her feet. "Being a husband and a father would cramp your life-style."

Pain flickered in his eyes. She'd hurt his feelings. Her chest ached. She felt his pain as though it were her own. For his sake, she couldn't allow herself to stop. Eric had to give up this foolhardy notion of wanting to marry her.

"I'll admit, I don't know much about being a father. But you're talking about material things. Things I can change."

She raised a brow. "What about the things you can't change?"

He frowned. "Like what?"

"Like your attitude toward marriage. Are you telling me you believe marriage is forever?"

"For some people." He refused to meet her eyes.

"But not for you," she added for him, her voice quiet.

His wordless answer spoke volumes.

"If I ever do marry again, it'll be for the same reason I married David. Because I want to spend a lifetime loving that person."

"Rest of your life? Or theirs? We're talking about a lot different time frame here, aren't we?"

She drew in a sharp breath, feeling as if she'd been slapped.

A look of regret crossed his face. "I'm sorry, Lily. That was out of line. I'm just a sore loser taking my frustration out on you." He rose to his feet. "You married David for love. You could marry me for the hell of it. No strings. No pain. I can't guarantee it'll last forever, but it'll be a whole lot of fun."

She shook her head. "Thanks, but no thanks."

"I'm not giving up," he said, his voice holding a hint of challenge. "I'm going to change your mind, Lily. One of these days you're going to admit you need me."

"You'll be wasting your time."

He drew her into his arms and kissed her soundly.

The room felt as though it were spinning when he finally released her.

"Wasting my time? Not hardly." With a satisfied grin, he left.

Hearing the click of the front door as he closed it behind him, she collapsed into the cushions of the sofa. Marriage for the hell of it. She sighed. Eric never ceased to amaze her.

What amazed her, as well, was her reaction to his proposal. For a moment, she'd been tempted to say yes. Her body still tingled with the memory of Eric's smoldering caress. She had no doubt, being married to Eric would be...interesting.

Guilt touched her heart. In David's arms, she'd felt safe and secure. In Eric's, she felt as though her world were spinning out of control. With a single touch, Eric could set her pulse racing and her body sizzling. She'd never felt that way with David. Somehow the realization left her feeling unfaithful to his memory.

Eric's caresses had put a crack in the wall she'd built around her heart, leaving her raw and unprotected. She drew up her legs, hugging them. Undeniable attraction aside, Eric had proposed to her out of a sense of obligation. They weren't in love. They were in lust. Whether or not her curse had anything to do with it, marriage to Eric would not last.

The thought chilled her. She pulled her arms tighter.

Eric was wrong. Being married wasn't fun.

Marriage always left its mark of pain.

Chapter Seven

Nine o'clock the next morning, Eric rang the doorbell of Lily's ranch. It was already a blistering ninety degrees outside. He could feel waves of heat radiating from the ground beneath his feet. A green speckled lizard skittered across the sidewalk, finding a shady spot beneath a rock. Eric sighed. Even a lizard knew when to get in out of the heat.

He wiped the perspiration from his brow with the back of his hand, then he glanced at his watch. A full minute had passed with no answer. Eric felt a niggling of impatience. Lily was home. Her car was in the driveway. He couldn't help but wonder if she was still trying to avoid him.

As quick as it surfaced, he nixed the idea. Last night they'd reached an understanding. He was going to convince her to marry him, and she was going to do her best to discourage him. The most stubborn of the two would win. He'd admit—it wasn't the most ideal understanding. But it was an understanding nonetheless.

Eric glanced at his watch again. A disturbing image of Lily almost fainting in the bakery cropped up in his mind. He shifted, one foot to the other. Lily told him she was feeling better. But what if she'd lied to keep him from worrying? What if she was sick? Or had fallen? Or was lying unconscious on the floor...?

Eric leaned on the doorbell.

Minutes later, the door opened. Eric glanced at the towel wrapped turban-style around Lily's head, the short terry-cloth bathrobe that hit her midthigh and the fuzzy slippers on her feet. Her skin was damp. Droplets of water clung to her neck and collarbone. Obviously he'd interrupted Lily's shower.

He wondered what she had on underneath her robe. The thought made him smile. "Did I catch you at a bad time?"

She glared at him. "Eric, what are you doing here? It's..." She glanced at her bare wrist, as though checking her wristwatch. Coming up empty-handed, she scowled. "It's early. Too early."

He held out a pastry box. "I brought you breakfast. Bran muffins."

"Thank you," she said, grabbing the box. "Now, go away."

"Come on, Lily." He gave her his most endearing smile. "I drove all the way over just to see you. Let me in."

"You drove all the way over just to check up on me. Next time, call first." She started to close the door.

His foot got in the way. "I thought maybe you'd like to do something with me today. How about a drive to the mountains? It'd sure be a lot cooler."

"I've already made plans."

"What kind of plans?"

She lifted her chin. "Not that it's any of your business, but I'm spending the day cleaning out the spare bedroom. I need the room for a nursery."

A nursery—for the baby. An unexpected surge of emotion rose in his chest. Eric took a deep breath. "That shouldn't take a whole day."

She frowned. "You're right. I'm probably underestimating. It may take two or three days."

He smiled. "How messy can a spare bedroom be?"

"Very messy. I've got papers to throw away. Boxes to sort through—"

"Boxes? That settles it. I'm helping. You shouldn't be lifting boxes in your condition."

"My condition?" She gave him a disgusted look. "You make it sound as though I have an incurable disease. I'm only pregnant, Eric."

He pushed his way past her into the house. "No arguments, Lily. I'm staying."

She followed him into the kitchen. "You can't barge into my house and give me orders. Besides, cleaning out a spare bedroom is dull, tedious work. Surely you have something better to do today."

"Nope." He took the pastry box from her hands, sat down at the kitchen table and withdrew one of the jelly doughnuts he'd bought for himself. "Cleaning house sounds fine to me."

She gave a strangled groan of frustration.

He took a bite of doughnut and glanced up at her. He froze midchew. Somewhere on the way to the kitchen, she'd lost the towel. Her hair fell in damp tendrils about her shoulders. The belt cinching the terry-cloth robe around her waist had loosened. Desire slammed into him, quick and hard, as he caught a teasing hint of creamy-white skin.

Slowly he swallowed the doughnut. "Um, Lily? Move another inch and you may be losing more than just your temper."

Her eyes followed the direction of his gaze. A rosy glow of embarrassment bloomed on her face as she clutched together the lapels of her robe. "Finish your doughnut, then go." She backed out of the room. "I mean it, Eric. I don't need your help."

Eric chuckled. Leave? When things were getting interesting? Not hardly.

While she was still dressing, he ate another doughnut and pondered the turnabout in his feelings for Lily. Last night he'd proposed a marriage with no strings attached. He'd lied. If he married her, his heart would be tangled in a web of emotions so thick he might never find his way out. Holding Lily, kissing her, had been magic. He'd never felt like this about another woman. It hurt to know she didn't feel the same way.

But if he admitted how deep his feelings ran, Lily would bolt from him as quick as a roadrunner disappearing into the desert brush. Eric sighed. One thing these past few weeks had taught him—he couldn't live without Lily in his life.

She asked if he thought marriage meant forever. There was a time when he'd believed in forever. Now he wasn't sure. She said he'd make a lousy husband. He was determined to prove her wrong.

If only he didn't blow it by going overboard. Since she'd become pregnant, he'd felt an uncharacteristic need to take care of her, to protect her. He'd become a man possessed. He was smothering her with attention.

Eric always considered himself fairly liberated when it came to women. He didn't have a choice. If he'd even considered women the weaker of the sexes, his sisters would have clobbered him. In his line of work, he dealt with many divorced, working mothers raising their children alone. He admired their determination to succeed and respected their seemingly endless number of capabilities.

But Lily was different. She'd always been different. One look into Lily's large green eyes turned him into a macho jerk. She made him do stupid things. Like yell at her for not taking care of herself when she fainted, when he really wanted to hold her in his arms and tell her how frightened he'd been. Eric sighed. Or push his way into her house uninvited when he'd awoken from a restless sleep and his first thoughts had been of her.

Two hours later, Eric glanced across the spare bedroom at Lily. Her mood had improved once she'd dressed and put food in her tummy. With a little persuasion, she'd reconsidered and allowed him to stay.

"You know, Lily," he said, "my house is big. It's got lots of empty rooms. If you married me, you wouldn't have to waste a whole day cleaning out this bedroom."

"Eric—" Her voice held a warning note.

He grinned. "Just a thought."

She didn't look amused.

Macho jerk, he muttered, moving away. He feigned interest in an open box. Lily made him do stupid things, all right. Like propose marriage every time he got within five inches of her.

Eric scowled. He knew Lily well enough to realize no one could force her to do anything she didn't want to do. He needed to slow down. They'd been friends for a long time. This attraction they felt for each other was new, its intensity frightening. Uncertainty shadowed Lily's face every time he was near. Instead of coming on strong and fast like a Mack truck, he needed to give her time to adjust to the idea of marrying him.

He had time. Admittedly, not much. Only seven months to convince her she needed him. And as hard as it might be, he would have to keep his hands in his pockets whenever she was close for as long as it took to prove he was serious, that his intentions were honorable. For as long as it took for her to say yes to his marriage proposal.

"Tell me about the curse," he said, steering the conversation to safer grounds.

Lily peered at him from around the corner of a box. "What do you want to know?"

"Everything."

"Why?"

"I want to know what I'm up against."

She stood slowly, stretching her legs. Her cutoffs gloved her curves. The material of her pink tank top strained against her breasts as she arched her back. Her movements were unaffected, guileless.

But the way his body reacted was anything but innocent. His mouth went dry. His heart pumped overtime. His blood ran hot and thick, sending urgent messages of arousal to points southward. Eric gritted his teeth and reminded himself of his honorable intentions.

"Still think you can talk me out of believing in my curse?" she asked.

Sweat beaded on his forehead as he struggled for control. "I told you, I don't give up easily."

"The curse has hung in there for over four generations of our family. It doesn't give up, either." She frowned, eyeing him curiously. "Are you sure you aren't getting overheated? You look a little flushed. Maybe you need a drink."

His gaze rested on the curls of hair escaping from her ponytail and clinging to the dewy, smooth skin on the back of her neck. He was thirsty, all right, but not for liquid nourishment.

"I'm fine," Eric said through clenched teeth. He was in deep trouble. This working-around-the-house stuff wasn't so bad. In fact, he was beginning to like it . . . too much. He jerked open the closet door. Then jumped back as boxes fell out to greet him.

Lily giggled. "Watch out, Eric. You never know what might pop out at you."

Feeling foolish always made him ornery. "Oh, yeah? Whatcha got in there, Lily? A skeleton or two?"

Her chin jutted out. "No, but there might be a spider. Black widows love the desert."

He chuckled, feeling the tension melt from his muscles. He'd discovered something new about Lily. She was a pack rat. Yearbooks from high school, photos of family vacations, outdated business files from the bakery and much more were crammed into her spare bedroom. The woman never threw anything away. He picked up a box. "What's in this thing? It's gotta weigh a ton."

Lily shrugged. "Probably old recipe books, or maybe some of my text books from college."

He placed the box at her feet. "Lily, you can't keep everything. You've got to learn to be ruthless, or all this stuff's going to take over your house."

She sighed as she knelt beside the box and opened the flaps. "I have a problem with getting rid of things. Every time I try, I freeze. I think, what if I need this someday?

Or if someone went to the trouble of buying me a gift, how could I possibly throw it away?"

He smiled at her sentimental logic. "Believe me, Lily, I don't think you'll be needing all those Pet Rocks." He moved away. "And that bottle opener in the shape of a duck. It's cute, but its bill is broken—"

Lily gasped.

Eric's heart leaped into his throat. In two quick strides, he returned to her side. "Are you okay? You didn't try to lift that box, did you? I told you not to lift anything heavy."

"I'm fine." Her face was pale. Her lips were trembling. She wasn't fine.

Eric knelt beside her. "Lily, what's wrong?"

"David." She swallowed hard. "These were David's."

Eric dropped his gaze to the box. Law books, business files, paper clips, an address book, desk calendar. His chest tightened. He didn't need to look any further. He recognized the contents. After David had died, Eric had been the one to clear out his desk at work. He was the one who had brought this box, with its memories of David, home for Lily.

A tear spilled down her cheek, making a damp spot on the cardboard lid. "After he died, I couldn't bear to look at his things. So I put away the box. I gave away his clothes to charity, but I forgot this was still in the closet."

Eric sat back on his heels. He hadn't thought about his friend since learning Lily was pregnant. Now, seeing her painful reaction to David's things triggered his memory and a flood of guilt. Guilt because, for the first time in his life, he was jealous of another man. A man who'd been dead for three years.

He closed the flap. "Let me take care of this for you," he said gruffly. "I'll cart the box home and sort through it. If there's something I think you'd want to keep, I'll bring it over."

Lily nodded.

He hesitated. "Lily, I want you to know something. During the time you were with David, I never once had a carnal thought about you."

Lily blinked. "I know that, Eric."

"You were my best friend's wife. I'd never have done anything to break his trust or yours."

"Of course you wouldn't." She frowned. "Eric, why are you telling me this now?"

Because I feel guilty as hell for wanting my best friend's wife. Especially since she still loves and cares for him more than she'll ever care for me. He shrugged. "I just wanted to make sure you knew, that's all."

She wiped away a tear with the back of her hand. "Eric, you have nothing to feel guilty about. If anyone does, it's me."

He released a slow breath. "I sure hope you're not talking about that curse again."

"No, not the curse." She shook her head. "Losing David was terrible. It hurt so bad. I thought I'd never be able to forget the pain. But lately I've been so wrapped up in my pregnancy I'd almost forgotten."

"David would want you to get on with your life."

"I know that." Her breath caught. "I just didn't think I could ever be happy again."

Relief washed over him, making him feel worse. "Are you happy, Lily?"

His heart did a flip-flop when she smiled up at him, her mouth soft and inviting. "Oh, yes, Eric. I'm very happy."

Warning signals pulsed throughout his body. He was dangerously close to pulling Lily into his arms and making love to her on the floor of her spare bedroom. His gut instinct stopped him. Now wasn't the time for romance.

He stood. "I'll put this in the car," he said, scooping up the box and moving away from temptation.

Lily sighed. "Now's as good a time as any for a break. How does a cold drink sound?"

He forced a smile. "Sounds great."

Not as good as holding her in his arms or kissing her. But a cold drink would have to do.

Mesmerized, Lily watched the cords of Eric's throat tighten and relax as he drank a glass of lemonade. As she sat next to him at the kitchen table, a delicious warmth stirred in the pit of her stomach, spreading waves of heat throughout her body.

She took a hasty sip of her own drink.

What was wrong with her? She was supposed to be keeping Eric safely at arm's length. But all she could think of was how nicely muscled his legs were beneath his black jogging shorts. She licked the lemonade from her lips. How tempted she was to run her fingers beneath his T-shirt and feel the hard muscles of his chest and—

"Aren't you forgetting something?" he asked.

She blushed, wondering if he could read her mind. "Excuse me?"

"The curse?" He smiled. "You were going to reveal the mystery behind your family's curse."

"Oh, that." Her muscles relaxed. "There's no mystery. Just your average curse starting with the wrath of a woman scorned."

Eric humphed. "Now, that I can believe."

"Don't spout your cynical divorce-attorney logic to me, Eric Mitchell. This time the woman wasn't to blame. My great-grandfather was at fault."

"Your great-grandfather?"

Lily nodded. "Great-grandpa O'Toole, born in Old Country Ireland. He was a handsome devil." A smile teased her lips. "Just like you, Eric, he liked to play fast with the ladies."

He scowled. "What did love 'em and leave 'em O'Toole do to deserve a curse?"

She shrugged. "He jilted the wrong woman. He became engaged to Pageen Rourke, but stepped out on her with my great-grandmother. When the two of them ran off and married, Pageen put a curse on our family." She sighed dramatically to emphasize her point. "Great-grandpa O'Toole never lived to see the day Nana was born."

"You mean this whole thing is over a broken engagement?" He gave her an incredulous look.

"In those days, it was a scandal. Of course everyone blamed my great-grandmother. After Great-grandpa O'Toole died, the poor woman was shipped off to America to live with an aunt."

"I don't get it," he said, frowning. "I could understand Pageen being a bit miffed, but what's the disgrace? Your great-grandparents were married, weren't they?"

She squirmed in her seat. "Well, yes—but after the fact."

The ends of his mouth curved into an amused grin. "Are you telling me your great-grandparents anticipated the wedding night?"

She glared at him. "Nana was a bit premature, that's all."

"How much premature?"

"Three months."

He hooted with laughter. Tears of mirth rolled down his cheeks. Eric appeared thoroughly amused at her family's expense and showed no sign of letting up.

Lily sat in her chair, simmering, waiting for him to stop.

He wiped a tear from his eye. "Sorry, Lily. Tell me the rest. What's the secret?"

"Secret?"

"The secret—the key to breaking the curse."

She frowned. "There isn't any. We're just stuck with it."

"Come on, Lily. Haven't you read your fairy tales? When the wicked witch places a curse on the undeserving princess, along comes a prince to break the spell."

She gave him a disgusted look. "This isn't a fairy tale, Eric. This really happened. Besides, true love is what breaks the spell in fairy tales. The women in my family have always loved their husbands. I think love is what killed them."

He considered this for a moment. "Maybe love isn't enough."

"What do you mean?"

"According to Grimm, the prince has to prove his love by doing something unselfish...and usually very stupid."

She laughed. "What makes you such an expert on *Grimm's Fairy Tales?*"

"My mother read us a story every night before we went to bed. Of course, I would have preferred a Western or a superhero comic book, but my sisters outnumbered me." He smiled at the memory. "It was either listen to fairy tales or nothing."

Lily caught the softening tone of his voice. Despite his grumblings, she had a feeling Eric had cared very deeply for his family. That he still cared. "Your mother sounds like a very special woman."

His smile became wistful. "Yes, she is. She worked hard after Dad died. She waitressed a twelve-hour shift to keep all of us fed."

"Did she ever remarry?"

He shook his head. "No, she never did. She always said a love like hers and Dad's came around once in a lifetime. She didn't need to settle for second best when she'd had perfection."

Lily felt a pang of envy for the love Eric's parents must have shared. Her mother and grandmother seemed content in their widowhood, also. Guiltily, she wondered if her love for David had been stronger, maybe she wouldn't be yearning for something that couldn't be hers. "How about your sisters? Are any of them married?"

"Yep, all of them." He grinned. "Can you believe it? I've got six nieces. Not a boy in the bunch."

Lily smiled. Girls, it seemed, ran in Eric's family, too. She wondered what it was like being a member of a big family. Probably not as lonely as being an only child.

Lily gave herself a mental shake. She was treading on dangerous ground, she warned herself. Start wondering about the family behind the man and she'd find herself getting too close to the man himself.

"I think you'd better stick to law briefs and leave the fairy tales to me," she said, sighing. "Believe me, Eric, there's nothing you or I can do to break the curse."

A mischievous glint lit his eyes. "At least now I know one thing."

She was almost afraid to ask. "What's that?"

"Where all that hot-blooded passion of yours comes from," he said, raising his brows suggestively. "You come by it naturally. Thanks to good ol' Grandpa O'Toole."

Embarrassment heated her face. She pushed herself from the table, rising to her feet. "I think it's time for you to leave, Eric."

He stood, catching her wrist. "I'm sorry, Lily." He pulled her snug against him, wrapping both arms around her waist, his hips nuzzling her fanny. "You looked so serious. I just wanted to make you smile."

She didn't say a word. She didn't dare move. She couldn't. For the past three years, she'd led a quiet, almost nunlike life. The feel of Eric's body pressed against hers left her weak with desire and her mind reeling with unspoken implications. A flood of sensual emotions threatened to overwhelm her.

"Tell me you forgive me," he said.

His breath was warm against her skin. A shiver ran down her spine as his lips touched her neck. She moaned. Maybe she was approaching this problem with Eric the wrong way. She'd adopted a hands-off policy, hoping to change his mind about wanting to marry her. So far, her plan hadn't met with much luck. If anything, he'd become even more relentless.

Eric thrived on a challenge. He was like a predator after his prey. He was the hound—she was the fox. He'd set his sights on her. Maybe she should just let him catch her.

"I forgive you," she said, wincing at the husky sound of her voice.

He hesitated a moment, then released her.

He let her go?

She swung around to face him. "You can stay if you promise not to mention a word about my family's curse."

He held up his hand. Three fingers, a Boy Scout oath. "I swear, my lips are sealed."

She studied him, chewing on her lower lip. "Okay, then let's get back to work."

"Fine."

"Fine?"

He was agreeing with her?

Eric looked confused.

"Just like that?" Had she misread that kiss on her neck? Maybe he'd noticed the blemish on the end of her nose, the one she'd woken up to this morning? Or maybe it was the extra couple of pounds she'd gained since becoming pregnant that was turning him off. "No arguments?"

His gaze was wary. "Is there something wrong?"

She forced a smile. "What could be wrong?"

"Nothing. I just thought—"

"Thought what? That I'd be upset because you find me unattractive?"

"Unattractive?"

"Don't be embarrassed, Eric. It's a known fact. Some men are turned off by pregnant women."

"You think I'm turned off?"

"I don't blame you. I know I've gained some weight."

He raked a gaze up and down her body. "Where?"

"Hormones are having a picnic with my body." She plunged on, driven by a need to purge herself of her prenatal insecurities. "My hair is losing its curl. My face looks like a minefield, one blemish exploding after another. I'm not afraid to admit the truth. I'm just plain—"

"Nuts!"

Eric grabbed her around the waist and pulled her against him. His kiss was demanding, thorough. When he released her, she felt weak and wobbly inside. "Now, do you still think I find you unattractive?"

"No," she said, shaking her head.

"Good." He placed his finger under her chin. "Let's get back to work before I forget I'm an honorable man and decide to take advantage of you after all."

Chapter Eight

"Maybe this was a mistake," Lily said.

Eric dropped his hand. He'd been checking his watch again. The third time in as many minutes. "Don't be silly. I don't mind waiting."

"You're lying. I know you have a full day of work at the office."

"If there was a problem, I'd tell you."

Two weeks had passed since he'd helped Lily clean out the spare bedroom. Two weeks of sheer torture.

Eric picked up a magazine and settled himself a notch lower in the tweedy gray chair. The chairs in the doctor's waiting room were packed closely together. As he moved, his elbow pillowed against the softness of Lily's breast. The touch felt like heaven. A hearty dose of ill-timed longing pulsed through his veins.

Lily, not so gently, shoved his elbow out of her way.

Sighing, he repositioned himself in his chair. He couldn't seem to control himself around her. While Lily was preparing herself for a doctor's visit, he was undressing her in his mind. He should be ashamed of himself.

But he wasn't.

Eric's body shouted a protest as he recalled the night he'd almost made love to Lily on her living-room couch and, more recently, the kiss they'd shared in her kitchen. On both occasions, he could have taken what she'd been so willing to offer. But, no. He'd had to give in to an unexpected bout of conscience. Like a fool, he'd decided to wait until she agreed to marry him.

Now he was the one paying the price. Every time he looked at her, touched her, he found himself wanting her more and more. He had no one but himself to blame for his misery. He slouched in his chair.

"Is the doctor always this behind in his schedule?" he asked, casting an impatient glance around the crowded room.

"Well..." Lily scrunched her eyebrows thoughtfully in an unsuccessful attempt to appear innocent. "I did have to wait awhile for my last visit."

Eric studied her for a long moment. When she'd asked him to drive her to an appointment with the doctor, he'd seen this as a step in weakening her resolve to remain unfettered by marriage. Finally, he had thought, Lily was beginning to realize that she needed him.

As usual, he was wrong. Lily didn't need him. In her subtle way, she was trying to prove a point. The point being, he wasn't cut out for the duties of a husband.

And Eric was beginning to think she was right.

He felt guilty leaving work during the middle of the day. He felt uncomfortable sitting in a doctor's waiting room filled with pregnant women. He felt frustrated and peeved with Lily for forcing him into this situation. But he'd be damned if he'd let his true feelings show. Lily wasn't going to be able to say "I told you so" this time.

"I should be next," she said. "All the other women came in after us."

Eric threw the magazine onto the rose-colored Formica end table. "I need to give my office a call. Let them know I won't be much longer."

"I feel awful about this, Eric. I had no idea we'd have to wait so long." She placed a hand on his arm.

Eric felt an instant jolt of desire.

"Maybe I should phone a taxi to pick me up, so you can go back to work."

"A taxi?" he mumbled, confused for a moment. The way his body was reacting, she might have been suggesting they leave for an afternoon of passion and pleasure. He gritted his teeth. "You haven't eaten in almost twelve hours while you've waited for this lab test. That's a record for you, Lily. Why do you think the doctor advised you to have someone else drive? You'll probably pass out from hunger if someone's not keeping an eye on you."

"I'm not that weak." She scowled.

He stood. "I'm staying. End of argument."

Eric strode to the pay phone near the entrance of the clinic and made a hurried call to his secretary. When he returned, he found the nurse already talking to Lily. He joined them quietly, catching bits of the conversation.

Lily shook her head and said, "No, I'm sure he wouldn't want to do that."

"He wouldn't want to do what?" Eric asked.

Lily jumped. As he'd suspected, she hadn't known he was there.

The nurse gave him an assessing glance. "I was asking Mrs. Gerard if you'd like to sit in on the ultrasound."

"I already told her you wouldn't be interested," Lily said.

"I understand." The nurse turned to Lily, excluding him from the conversation. "Most men are a little hesitant when it comes to tests involving the birthing process. Maybe some other time."

Lily and the nurse exchanged knowing smiles.

He could almost read their minds. They were chucking him off as a squeamish, weak-kneed male. Irritation took the place of common sense. He hadn't been waiting for the past hour and fifteen minutes just to be passed over. If there was something he could do, then by God, he was going to do it.

"Mrs. Gerard's wrong," he announced, looking Lily squarely in the eye. "I'd be thrilled to sit in on the ultrasound."

Lily's mouth dropped open.

"That's wonderful." The nurse gave him an approving nod. "I'll be out for you as soon as Mrs. Gerard is ready."

Lily shot him a prohibitive glance.

Eric smiled.

With a swing of her auburn hair, Lily turned and left.

Eric collapsed into his chair. What in the world was he thinking of? He had a very low tolerance for anything that involved pain. The sight of blood made him queasy. When he'd sprained his ankle last year playing baseball, he'd nearly passed out during the X-ray. He couldn't watch an ultrasound. He frowned. What was an ultrasound? He gave an involuntary shudder. Whatever it was, it sounded ominous.

Minutes later, the nurse returned. Eric's feet felt like lead as he followed her to the examining room. Silently he cursed his big mouth and the trouble it always seemed to get him into.

Lily was lying on the examining table, wearing a hospital gown. The lower half of her body was discreetly swathed in a green sheet.

"Have a seat." The lab technician motioned to a stool at the head of the table.

Lily's irritable mood had changed. She looked uneasy, almost glad to see him. She gave him a tentative smile.

He grinned in return, determined not to let his own nervousness show.

"Ready?" the technician asked. Not giving them a chance to answer, he moved the sheet and squirted a clear gel on Lily's stomach.

Lily jumped reflexively.

Eric flinched. "Does it hurt?"

Lily shook her head. "It's as cold as ice."

Instinctively Eric picked up her hand, warming it in his. He shot the technician a glowering look. "You could have warned her," he snapped.

The technician appeared surprised. "Sorry, I just didn't think..." He gave Lily an apologetic glance. "The rest of the ultrasound is painless. I promise."

"It'd better be," Eric growled.

Lily squeezed his hand. "It's okay, Eric."

His reaction had been quick and unexpected. He'd acted on gut instinct to protect her. Now he felt a bit foolish. "Sorry, Lily."

The technician dimmed the lights and directed their attention to something that looked like a grainy TV screen. Eric kept a wary eye on the technician as he slowly glided a wand over Lily's exposed stomach. Then he studied the screen, his gaze skeptical. Lily wasn't quite ten weeks pregnant. He didn't expect to be able to see much.

He was wrong.

The screen came alive with a pulsing movement. He felt himself leaning forward to get a closer look. "What in the world is that?"

"That's the baby, Eric," Lily said, sounding amused.

The technician pointed at the screen. "See that? That's the heart."

A lump of emotion lodged in his throat. He swallowed hard, trying his best to concentrate on the screen. Until that moment, he'd thought of the baby as an extension of Lily, not alive with a heart of his or her own.

Lily asked the technician questions about the baby's position and size.

Eric watched and listened, too overwhelmed to speak. With each grainy image flickering across the screen, he saw a baby develop before his eyes. Slowly he realized Lily was more than just pregnant.

She was carrying his child.

"I think it's a boy," Eric said, squinting at the black-and-white photo he held in his hand.

"It's too early to tell the baby's sex by ultrasound, Eric. Today's test was just to determine whether the pregnancy is viable and if the baby's in the correct position."

Eric leaned across the restaurant table and pointed to a large blob on the photo. "This kid's endowed." He winked. "He takes after his father."

Lily nearly choked on her western omelette.

Before her doctor's visit, Eric had squirmed in his chair, dropping hints that he was wasting valuable time as he waited for the doctor. He'd looked ready to renege on his responsibilities and run at a moment's notice. She had felt content knowing that her intuition was right. Eric had only needed a gentle nudge to show him he wasn't ready for fatherhood.

But all that changed after the ultrasound. She'd been nervous about the test, worried they might find something wrong with the baby. Then Eric had joined her. He'd been kind and gentle, a calming strength. She'd been relieved to have him with her. She had to admit—seeing her baby for the first time with Eric at her side had been special.

When they'd finished at the doctor's office, Eric had insisted on taking her out for breakfast. She'd reminded him of his duties at the office, but he'd waved off her concern, saying he had all day to work. Now, sitting across the table from her at the diner, he was raving about the ultrasound picture and acting like a typical expectant father.

"Eric, whether *the kid's endowed* is impossible to determine at this stage," she said, feeling her temper flare. "Besides, the *kid* is a girl, not a boy."

He frowned. "How do you figure that?"

"My family always has girls. It's part of the curse."

He snorted his disbelief.

Irritation shot through her veins. "It makes more sense than you pointing to a spot on the photo and proclaiming it's a boy."

"Sounding a bit tetchy, aren't we, Lily?" Eric scooted his untouched plate of toast toward her. "Have something more to eat."

She grabbed the plate with the intention of returning it, but their fingers linked on the rim. A sensual rush of heat swept her body. She remembered the way his hand had felt holding her, caressing her. Lily clenched her teeth. One touch and he had her quivering inside. She had the backbone of a jellyfish, she chastised herself silently.

"Stop treating me like a child," she said, dropping her hand from the plate.

"Then stop acting like one," he countered.

Their eyes met across the width of the table.

The waitress chose that moment to warm their coffee. She snapped her gum. "Need some more bacon? Or how about another glass of juice?"

"No," they answered simultaneously, their eyes still deadlocked in a battle of wills.

"Uh-huh." The gum snapped again. "Well, have a nice day." She slapped the bill on the table and scurried back to the kitchen.

"Happy, Eric? You just scared that poor girl."

"Me? I'm not the one who started this." He pointed a finger at her. "You did."

When she refused to answer, he leaned toward her in a confiding manner. "What's the matter, Lily? Experiencing one of those mood swings of pregnancy I've been reading about?"

"You've been reading about?" She threw her napkin on the table. "Why would you want to read up on pregnancy?"

"So I can figure out what's wrong with you, that's why," he shouted, ignoring the stares they were receiving from their fellow diners. "One minute you're sweet as honey, the next you act as though you took a bite out of a lemon. Help me out here, Lily. I don't know how to act around you."

She drew in a shaky breath. "You don't have to act, Eric. If you're uncomfortable, stop spending time with me."

"You're the one who asked me to drive you today."

"Obviously that was a mistake."

"Why? Because I didn't react the way you thought I would?"

His question took her by surprise.

"Admit it, Lily. You were hoping I'd shirk my responsibilities and hightail it back to the office at the first sign of a problem, weren't you?"

She averted her eyes. His assumption came too close to the truth.

"Well, thank you for your high regard of my character," he said, his voice steeped in sarcasm. "I guess this throws a kink in your theory that I'm not ready for marriage, doesn't it?"

She caught her breath. Eric had scored a direct hit. What she felt for him went beyond mere physical attraction. He had proved himself to be concerned and responsible. Lily felt herself turning to him more and more for support. The realization left her shaken. For the first time in years, she felt her resolve to stay commitment-free slipping away.

She clambered to her feet. "I have to go back to work."

He stood to join her. "At least you made it through an entire meal before deciding to run away this time, Lily," he said, his voice low and taunting.

The remark cut deep. She crossed her arms, curbed her temper and waited as he paid the bill. The short drive to the bakery was quiet, the car rife with tension.

Eric pulled his car into a parking spot. Lily scrambled out. Waves of suffocating heat rose up from the pavement to meet her, taking her breath away. She clutched the car door for support.

Eric came around, putting a hand on her shoulder. "Look, we both said things in anger. Why don't we just forget it and start over?"

She shrugged, forcing him to drop his hand. "Under the circumstances, I think it'd be better if we didn't see each other for a while, Eric."

"You're kidding, right?"

"I have a baby to consider. All this tension between us can't be good for my pregnancy."

Looking stunned, he stepped away.

Heat, having more to do with guilt than the weather, flushed her body. She felt terrible. She was using her pregnancy to hide from her inability to deal with her own feelings. But she couldn't bring herself to admit the truth to Eric—that she was beginning to care too much about him.

"Are you sure this is what you want?"

She swallowed hard. "It's the way it has to be."

He nodded, his face drained of all emotion. She yearned to wrap her arms around him and hold him tight, tell him not to believe anything she'd said. She fought the urge.

Without another word, he turned away.

Slowly Lily walked to the bakery. Regret and the heat made her steps sluggish. Her hurry to leave Eric's side was now forgotten. She licked her lips, tasting the salty flavor of her own tears.

She was halfway across the courtyard, when she heard the high-pitched squeal of tires. Then, seconds later, the sickening rasp of metal crunching against metal. She froze, glued to the spot by sheer panic.

Eric.

Eric stood to one side of his Porsche and stared, too numb to speak. The back end of his car looked like an accordion, folded in and squeezed tight.

However, the canary-yellow Lincoln Towne Car that had rammed into his car didn't have a scratch. He watched as an older woman, wearing a flowered dress, a straw sun hat and tan orthopedic shoes, pulled herself out of the driver seat.

"Oh, my," she said, examining the damage. "Looks as though we had a little bump."

"Little bump? Lady, you just backed into my car going thirty miles an hour."

She shrugged. "I didn't see it. That thing's so little, I thought the space was empty."

A crowd was beginning to gather around them. He gazed at her in concern. "Are you okay? You aren't hurt, are you?"

"Pish-posh, hurt? Not in my car." The woman patted the unblemished fender of her Lincoln. She narrowed her eyes at what was left of his Porsche. "Good thing your car was just a bitty thing. My insurance company might not have liked it if I'd hit something big."

His mother had taught him to be polite to his elders, no matter what the circumstances, but he was on his way to forgetting his lesson. "Ma'am, I don't think you understand—"

"Eric."

The breathless, haunting quality of the voice that said his name sent a chill down his spine. Eric turned. Lily stood on the sidewalk, appearing pale and scared.

"You're okay?" she asked, her eyes devouring him from head to toe.

"I'm fine," he said. He took a step toward her.

"I heard the crash. I thought you might have . . ." She gave a long shudder, then threw herself into his arms.

Sweet relief flooded through him. Moments ago his heart felt as though it had been ripped in two. He'd thought he'd lost Lily for good. But now she was back. He didn't care about the reason. "Lily, I'm okay." He felt the tremors shaking her body. He held her close, rocking her gently. "I'm okay."

"I don't know what I'd do if anything had happened to you."

"Nothing happened." He heard the tears choking her voice. For the moment, he forgot about his car. He forgot the people watching them and concentrated on Lily.

"I told you I was bad luck." Pushing herself from his arms, she looked at his car. Her face grew even paler. "You could have been killed."

He frowned, puzzled. "You think this was your fault?"

"Of course it was my fault. If it wasn't for me, you wouldn't be in this parking lot."

"Lily, if it wasn't for you, I'd have been in that car, not standing here on this sidewalk."

Slowly she shook her head. "I don't understand."

"You just told me I couldn't see you again. I was so angry, I didn't trust myself to drive. I was waiting for my temper to cool down, when…" He motioned to the older woman who was watching them curiously. "…she backed into my car."

Lily didn't seem convinced. "Eric, I don't think—"

"Don't you get it, Lily?" He chuckled, scooping her into a crushing embrace. "Your curse didn't almost kill me. It saved my life."

"Eric, I think you've been out in the sun too long." She shimmied out of his embrace and pressed a palm to his forehead. Her hand felt cool and reassuring against his feverish skin. "What about your car?"

His car. The only cloud in an otherwise perfect sunny day. "It can be fixed. If not, I needed a new car any-

way," he said, grinning like a fool. "Something not so fast
and expensive."

"Does this mean I won't have to report this little accident?" the older woman interrupted, looking hopeful.

"Ma'am, I may be acting a little strange, but I'm not
crazy." He dug into his back pocket for his wallet. "We've
got some serious talking to do. Let's start with insurance
cards."

"Thank goodness." Lily sighed, taking a step away.
"You're finally back to normal."

His jubilant spirit waned. "You can't leave now. Where
are you going?"

"Work, where else?"

"But what about the curse... about us?"

"There is no us, Eric," she said, without so much as a
blink. "I don't ever want to see you again."

"What?"

"Believe me, Eric. I'm doing this for your own good."
She motioned toward his car. "Next time, you may not be
so lucky."

"Lily, don't you dare walk out on me now. Lily—" He
watched with openmouthed astonishment as she strode
away without a backward glance.

"I love him."

Lily handed the dark-haired woman a tissue.

The young woman dabbed at the tears streaming down
her face, then blew her nose. "But I barely know him. He
swept me off my feet. We rushed into an engagement,
planned the ceremony, then found out we weren't compatible."

"Are you sure you're ready to cancel the wedding? Maybe you should give yourself more time," Lily suggested.

"More time?" The woman shook her head. "You don't understand. He wants us to live with his mother... permanently. He's thirty years old and hasn't moved out of his mother's house." New tears burst through. "I want a man, not a momma's boy."

Lily sat back in her chair, wondering what else could go wrong today. She'd left Eric and his wrecked car twenty minutes ago, and now this. A bride-to-be coming in to cancel her wedding cake didn't happen often, but when it did Lily felt the same way—sympathetic, yet terribly helpless.

She sensed a kindred spirit in this heartbroken woman. She knew how it felt to be disillusioned by love. Of course, her situation had been slightly different. She'd lost her husband's love when he'd died in a plane crash. But if it hadn't been for love in the first place, she'd never have had to suffer the pain following his death.

No love, no pain.

That had been her motto for the past three years. A creed that had served her well. Until recently, that is. Now she was beginning to think that no love meant no life.

She blamed Eric for her vacillation. Her chest tightened, swelling with rapidly rising panic. She'd thought having a baby would fill the void in her life. But Eric had made her realize she needed so much more.

When she'd left him in the parking lot, she'd told him she never wanted to see him again. But if Eric walked into the bakery right now, she would have a hard time turning him away. Lily gave a disgusted sigh. One look into his brown eyes and she'd be putty in his hands.

"If only I'd waited before saying yes to his marriage proposal," the bride-to-be moaned, drawing Lily out of her pensive thoughts. "I might have saved both of us a lot of trouble."

Lily nodded, realizing this was a lesson for her to keep in mind, as well. "This may be painful right now, but in the long run, you should be thankful you found out his true nature before the wedding. Think what might have happened if you'd discovered it after you were married."

"Yeah, me, Hank and Sylvia would be living happily ever after," the woman muttered. "Just one big, happy family."

Lily bit her lower lip to stop herself from smiling.

The bell chimed as the bakery door opened, catching Lily's attention. With his shirt sleeves rolled up and the knot on his tie loosened, Eric entered the bakery, looking angry. After a quick glance around the showroom, he zeroed in on her.

Lily's heart pounded. Her legs trembled as she got up, ending the conversation with the young woman. Lily ushered her out the door with a sympathetic goodbye, then turned to Eric.

He stood at the counter, watching her. His gaze traveled the length of her body, his brown eyes searing her like a fiery touch.

A spark of inner heat caught and smoldered inside her, threatening to burn out of control. She drew in a steadying breath, shaken by the sudden impact of these feelings. For Eric's sake, and her own, she couldn't allow him to know how much he affected her.

"How's your car?" she asked, hoping to sound casual. But she heard the strained pitch of her voice.

"The tow truck arrived a few minutes ago. The mechanic driving the truck doesn't think it's totaled. But it's going to be in the shop for a while."

"I'm sorry."

He shrugged. "There's nothing for you to be sorry about. I told you, if it wasn't for you—"

"I know, if it wasn't for me, you'd have been in that car, not standing on the sidewalk. But we both know the truth. I'm to blame, Eric."

He scowled, seemingly ready to argue. But to her surprise, the frown lines eased. A smile touched his lips.

"You're right. The accident was all your fault, Lily."

"What?"

"You'll just have to make it up to me."

She narrowed her eyes. Now what was he up to? "Exactly how am I supposed to do that?"

"I need a ride home to shower and change before I can go to work."

Lily surveyed him with a critical eye. Grease marks smudged his arms and shirt. His pants, which normally hung in sharp creases, were wrinkled and mussed. He wasn't lying. He appeared to have spent the past half an hour crawling under his car.

"Would you like for me to call you a taxi?" she asked, smiling sweetly.

"No," he said, his tone brooking no argument. "I want you to drive me."

Alone in a car with Eric. Alone with him in his home. She fought a rising tide of panic as she considered his request. She wasn't a weak-willed woman. She could handle a few moments alone with Eric without giving in to temptation. She would take him home, say goodbye, then never see him again.

Lily felt Eric watching her, waiting for her answer. Squaring her shoulders, she faced him with more determination than she actually felt. "You win, counselor. Since the accident was my fault, I'll give you a ride home. But that's as far as my obligation goes. After that, we don't see each other again. Is that understood?"

Eric's lips curved into a smile.

Lily felt her confidence slip. For a man who'd been firmly rejected, Eric looked and acted like a man who'd been given the upper hand.

Chapter Nine

"Do you think you could drive a little faster?"

Lily drew in a calming breath before answering. "Eric, you're the one who asked me for a ride. I'm just making sure you get home safe and sound."

"I could've walked faster."

Refusing to be pulled into a confrontation, Lily bit down the angry retort that rested on the tip of her tongue. She narrowed a glance at Eric. His face was drawn into a scowl. His eyes were dark like thunder.

Eric had been spoiling for a fight since they'd left the bakery. Once they were alone in her Volvo, he tried to convince her that her curse had nothing to do with his accident. But Lily had stood her ground. She'd remained steadfast in her belief that she'd been to blame for the accident.

Eric had been grumbling ever since.

Lily flicked on her blinker and slowly turned onto Eric's street. He lived in Paradise Valley, an affluent community outside of Phoenix, which had large, sprawling homes, neatly landscaped lots and a premium view of Camelback Mountain, a rocky mountain shaped like a camel.

Eric's move from his condo to a house last spring had surprised her. Especially since the house had four bedrooms, a big backyard and a family-sized pool. At the time, Lily had thought the house a tad large for a bachelor who had no intention of filling it with children.

She recalled his unexpected marriage proposal, and she sighed. Lately Eric seemed full of surprises.

She pulled the car into his driveway.

Eric swung open his door and got out.

Lily hesitated.

"You are coming in, aren't you?" he asked, peering at her from the open door.

She gripped the steering wheel. "You asked for a ride home. You didn't say anything about coming inside."

"How am I supposed to get to work? I don't have a car."

"I'm not your chauffeur, Eric." Her voice remained calm in the wake of his rising temper. "Call a taxi, rent a car—"

"I will as soon as I get to work," he said through clenched teeth. "Now, are you coming inside or not?"

Lily noted the determined look on his face. He wasn't going to give up without a fight. She was tired of arguing. With a resigned sigh, she turned off the ignition and got out of the car.

Palm fronds rustled in the quiet desert wind as she followed Eric to the front door. The sound reminded her of the clicking of disapproving tongues.

Click, click, click.

The intuitive voice in the back of her mind told her to turn around, get back into her car and drive away as fast as she could... before it was too late.

Lily pushed the thought away. She was acting like a person with a guilty conscience, when she'd done nothing wrong. She stole a glance at the wide strength of Eric's back and the tapering lines of his waist.

Click, click, click.

Oh, no. She hadn't done anything wrong.

Not yet, anyway.

A cool air-conditioned draft met her at the doorway, washing against her flushed skin. Lily shivered as she stepped into the foyer. The rooms were dark and still. Wooden shutters covered the windows, protecting the furnishings against the damaging rays of sunlight.

To the left was the living room. To the right, the dining room. Both rooms stood empty. Months ago, Eric had told her he intended to buy furniture for the rooms. Obviously he hadn't found the time. The empty rooms gave the house an uninhabited, lonely feel.

"I won't be long," Eric said, his tone curt as he headed down the hall to his bedroom.

"I could use a drink," Lily called after him.

"You know where the kitchen is," he answered, not bothering to look back.

Lily watched his long-legged strides eat up the carpeted floor. He disappeared into his bedroom and slammed the door, making it perfectly clear he was still angry.

Grumbling her frustration, Lily strode into the galley-style kitchen. She shot an irritable glance around the room. Her grandmother always said you could tell a lot about a man by the way he lived. Eric's kitchen appeared shiny and unused. She peered into the oven. Just as she had suspected, it was as spotless as a showroom sample.

The refrigerator, however, showed some signs of life. A quick inventory turned up a six-pack of imported beer with one bottle missing, a milk carton with an expiration date that had passed and a solitary orange collecting mold in the fruit drawer. She wrinkled her nose disdainfully. Evidently Eric didn't spend much time eating at home.

Her anger waned as her nurturing instincts kicked in. No man should live on take-out food from restaurants. Eric should have home-cooked meals and milk that wouldn't make him sick when he drank it. She smiled at the irony. All these weeks he'd been trying to convince her she needed him. When in truth, Eric needed someone to take care of him.

She closed the refrigerator door. Then she heard the crash of breaking glass. It took a moment for her to realize the sound hadn't come from inside the refrigerator. It had come from the opposite end of the house—from the bedroom. Imagining the worst, Lily sped from the kitchen and followed a muffled trail of expletives to Eric.

She hurried through his bedroom and caught a fleeting glance at the unmade king-size bed. Curbing the sensual fantasies racing through her mind, she reminded herself of her mission—checking on Eric's well-being. She found him in the master bathroom.

Undaunted by his scowling face, Lily scanned his body from head to toe, checking for damage. He was still dressed, but his unbuttoned shirt hung loose around his shoulders, revealing a matting of dark hair, the hard curves of his chest and the flat planes of his stomach. He looked sexy, handsome and, thankfully, unhurt.

The tension melted from her muscles. She went limp with relief, collapsing against the doorframe. Assured by his obvious good health, she noticed for the first time that he stood in a circle of shattered glass. "What in the world happened?"

"The mirror over the medicine cabinet broke," he muttered. He averted his eyes, not meeting her gaze.

"A broken mirror," she murmured thoughtfully. "Seven years bad luck."

He released a breath through clenched teeth, making an impatient whistling sound. "Don't start that again. I don't want to hear a word about curses or bad luck."

Lily squatted, picking up a chunk of broken mirror. "I don't have to say a word. It's obvious." She held up the jagged piece, staring into it as though it were a looking glass and she could see the future. A future marked with pain and unhappiness. "Someone or something is trying to warn us. We shouldn't be together."

"The only warning that mirror is giving is to cool my temper." He glared at her. "It didn't spontaneously leap from the wall, Lily. The mirror fell when I slammed my fist against the medicine cabinet. Your curse has nothing to do with it."

If his admission was meant to comfort her, it failed miserably. She felt worse. Her heart thudded painfully against her chest as she envisioned Eric angry and lashing out. The taut lines of Eric's face still echoed his anger and frustration.

Hot tears pressed against her eyes as she thought of what they were doing to each other. The pain. The anger. The frustration in wanting something they couldn't have. Somehow she had to stop the roller-coaster ride of emotions that they found themselves on before it was too late.

Still holding the broken glass, Lily stood. "Why can't you just accept it, Eric?"

"Accept what?" He stepped toward her, glass crunching beneath his feet.

Lily sucked in a sharp breath. She couldn't think clearly when he was near. Her mind and body warred in opposing directions, one urging her to walk away, the other wanting to stay. She back-stepped until she came up against the doorframe. "You have to accept the fact that I can't marry you."

Silently she chastised herself for her weak-sounding answer. She'd said—*can't*.

Not *won't*.

Not *I don't want to*.

Can't. As in, if circumstances were different, she would.

"I'll never accept that." He closed the distance between them.

Her grip tightened reflexively on the glass. Flinching, she dropped it.

Eric stood before her. Without a word, he took her hand and cradled it in his. Their eyes met and held. She told herself to move, but she couldn't muster the strength.

His gaze dropped to her hand. A drop of blood clung to a small cut on her palm. He drew in a ragged breath before raising her hand to his lips.

Lily shuddered as she felt the feathery touch of his tongue, the gentle sucking of his mouth on her wound. "Eric...don't."

"Don't what?" he murmured, his lips still against her palm. "Don't try to make the pain go away?"

He was talking about much more than just the cut on her hand. She wondered if he'd read her mind. Could he feel the pain in her heart, as well?

"Eric, please—"

"Please you," he said, nestling her hand against his cheek.

His skin felt warm and rough, with just the beginnings of a five o'clock shadow.

"Be with you. That's all I want. Don't shut me out, Lily. Not now."

She fought the shock wave of sensations his touch erupted inside her. "Eric, you don't know what you're getting yourself into."

"Wrong. I know exactly what I'm getting into, broken mirrors, wrecked cars, curses and all. None of those things has stopped me from wanting you. From wanting to marry you."

Lily sighed.

"I do want to marry you, Lily," he insisted. "Not because I have a guilty conscience to soothe. Or because I think you need someone to take care of you. But because I want to be with you."

She closed her eyes, steeling herself against the enticement of his voice. She felt the burn of unshed tears. Tears had been her constant companion since becoming pregnant. When she was happy, she cried. When she was tired, she cried. Now, when her heart felt as though it were being torn in two, she wanted to cry.

"Look at me, Lily."

She opened her eyes, her vision blurring. He stood before her, looking so strong and handsome, yet so terribly vulnerable.

"All I'm asking is for you to give me a chance. You think I'm poor husband material. I'll admit, I have a weakness for things that are fast and expensive. After my dad died my family was dirt poor. There were so many things we needed but couldn't afford. I swore when I grew up I'd never live that way again. And for the most part I haven't. But there's one thing I've learned in these past few months—having money can't buy you happiness. Being with you, Lily, would make me happy."

"Don't you understand? I'm afraid—" Her voice broke.

He cupped her chin in his palm, forcing her to meet his gaze. "You're afraid it won't last. I can understand that. I haven't had much luck with long-term relationships."

He took a deep breath as though preparing himself for a difficult task. She waited, curiosity keeping her silent.

"There's something I think you should know, Lily. Before I met you, when I first got out of law school, I was engaged."

She stared at him, stunned by his admission. She hadn't known what to expect, but this...nothing could have surprised her more.

Eric continued, his voice husky with emotion, "I was young and thought I was in love. Cynthia, that was her name, was rich and cultured. She represented everything that had been missing in my life. At first she found my impoverished background fascinating. But it didn't take long before the reality of marrying a struggling lawyer became too much for her." He released a harsh breath, averting his gaze. "She broke off our engagement when she found someone else, someone with a bigger bank account."

Her heart went out to him. "Oh, Eric..."

He brushed away her sympathy with an impatient shake of his head. "My heart recovered. But my pride took a hell of a beating. All these years I've been preaching the virtues of bachelorhood, when the truth is, the thought of making another commitment has me shaking in my shoes. I'm tired of being scared, Lily. I'm not going to let fear take away our chance at being together."

Lily leaned her head against the doorframe, her mind reeling with this new insight into Eric's life. All the years she'd known him, she'd believed him to be a charming womanizer. In truth, he was a man who'd been hurt deeply and was protecting his wounded pride. He'd taken a risk in asking her to marry him; she understood that now. Fresh tears welled up in her eyes. The thought of causing him more pain made her feel even worse.

"I wish it were that simple," she said. A single tear slipped down her cheek, followed by another.

He drew her toward him, his lips tracing the trail of tears. "It can't get any simpler. You're having my baby. And I care more about you than anyone else in the world. If you ask me, those are two damn good reasons to get married," he said, his voice barely a whisper. "I can't promise you forever, Lily. But I'm willing to take a stab at it." He gave a halfhearted grin. "Hell, I'll even throw out the prenupt, if you want. I'll do anything to prove I'm serious."

She studied him, her eyes wide and shimmering. "Eric Mitchell, beneath that cynical exterior, you have the soul of a romantic."

He frowned. "Does this mean you're accepting my proposal?"

"You make it hard to say no,' she said softly.

He grew impatient. "Lily, will you marry me?"

A shiver of desire, mixed with an equal amount of uncertainty, traveled the length of her body. Weeks ago she'd told Eric that if she married again, it would be because she wanted to spend a lifetime loving that person. Lily looked into his eyes—those beautiful brown eyes—and sighed.

Well, she loved him.

Before she'd asked him to father her child, she'd loved him as a friend. Now that love had changed. The rush of blind panic she'd felt when she thought he'd been hurt in a car accident had proved that.

Eric hadn't mentioned love in his proposal. He'd said he cared about her. Perhaps that was for the best. She was probably grasping at straws, but if Eric didn't love her . . . then maybe, just maybe, the curse wouldn't affect him as it had David.

The curse. Her muscles tensed. She was tired of the curse and the control it had over her life. In Eric's arms, she could almost believe nothing would hurt them. He made her want to love again. He made her want to feel loved.

With more confidence than she felt, Lily said, "Yes, Eric. Heaven help us, I'll marry you."

He stared at her for a long moment without speaking, feeling as though he couldn't believe what he'd just heard.

"It' s about time," he muttered. He pulled her against him, claiming her lips in an impatient kiss. Lily wrapped her arms around his waist and pressed her body against his.

His body reacted with a quickness that startled him. With a growl of primitive desire, Eric deepened the demands on her mouth. He tilted her head back and parted her lips with the brush of his tongue.

She returned his kiss with a feverish urgency.

New flames of desire exploded throughout his body, threatening to consume him. He tore his lips away and struggled for control. He wanted to make love to her. He wanted to be as close to her as any man could possibly be to a woman. But something was holding him back. Something was telling him that now wasn't the time.

So much about their relationship had been unconventional. Unconventional? Hell, they'd made a baby together even before he'd kissed her. Now, more than ever, was the moment to follow the rules of convention. The first time he made love to Lily, he wanted it to be special. He wanted it to be perfect. He wanted to wait until their wedding night.

"Lily," Eric murmured, groaning as she planted kisses across his cheek, his chin.

"Hmm?" she asked, tickling his ear with her breath. She slipped her hands beneath his shirt.

A new wave of heat flushed his skin. His mind might be telling him to slow down, but his body wanted to go sixty-five in a thirty-mile-an-hour zone. One more test of his willpower and he was going to fail miserably.

He caught her hands, holding them still. "Lily, we have to talk."

Lily glanced up at him. With her green eyes sparkling like emeralds, a bloom of healthy color on her cheeks, her lips pink and slightly swollen from his kisses, she looked beautiful and very desirable. Eric felt his body respond.

"I want to make love to you," he said, his voice a tortured whisper.

She smiled. "I want to make love to you, too."

"But not right now."

The smile faded. "I don't understand—"

"Let me explain," he said in a rush, before his courage ran out. "For the past couple of months, we've been doing everything backward. First you got pregnant. Then I proposed marriage." He sighed. "It was only after you turned me down that we kissed. Now that you've finally accepted my proposal, I'd like nothing more than to make love to you."

"So, what's the problem?"

"Call it old-fashioned, but I think we should wait until our wedding night."

The smile returned. "Don't you think it's a little late for tradition, Eric?"

"No, I don't. Up to this point, everything about our relationship has been nontraditional. That's why I think the first time we make love should be different."

She considered this for a moment, then asked, "Are you sure this isn't your way of making sure I go through with the wedding?"

"Maybe it is. But just remember, I have to wait, too. I'll be suffering right along with you."

"You never cease to amaze me, Eric."

"I never cease to amaze myself," he said with a grimace.

Lily sighed. "Okay, counselor, you win. We'll wait."

He kissed her. A gentle kiss rich with the promise of love. When they broke apart, Lily placed her head against his chest. He cradled her in his arms, relishing the closeness of the moment.

"So, how does Saturday sound to you?" he asked, breaking the silence.

"Sounds wonderful. I've got orders for three weddings and a bridal shower."

He growled his impatience. "I'm not talking about work—I'm talking about a date for our wedding."

"Our wedding?" An incredulous look glittered in her eyes.

"What? Too long of a wait? Then how about today?"

She was stunned. "Eric, we can't get married today."

"Why not? There's no waiting period in Arizona," he reminded her. "I know a judge who'd be willing to marry us this afternoon. All you have to do is say the word, and I'll give him a call."

Her lips curved into a smile, sending his heart racing.

"This judge, is he a friend of yours?"

"Not exactly."

Eric grinned, recalling the angry-faced judge. On numerous occasions, they'd butted heads in the courtroom. He remembered vividly the trial when the judge had lost his patience and pointed an accusing finger at him, telling him he couldn't wait for the day when Eric married. The judge bellowed he would like nothing more than to see Eric sweating it out on the other side of the divorce table. Eric decided this was not a memory he would care to share with Lily.

Lily sighed. "Well, it doesn't matter. Even Saturday would be too soon."

Eric didn't like her answer. "I'm not a strong man, Lily. I don't think I can wait much longer. Why can't we get married on Saturday?"

"Lots of reasons."

He persisted. "Name one."

"It's only four days away. It takes time to plan a wedding. Weeks, months."

Eric reached out and patted her tummy. "If you recall, our time is limited. We don't have months."

She brushed his hand away. "We can't plan a wedding until we've figured out a way to break the news to our families."

"*Break* the news? You make it sound as though it were bad news," he said. "My mother's been praying for this day."

"Oh?" Lily arched a brow. "What is she going to say when she finds out she's going to have a daughter-in-law and a grandchild all at the same time?"

"That she's double blessed. A grandson to carry on the Mitchell name is second on her list of prayers."

"Granddaughter," she corrected him with a teasing smile on her lips. As quickly as it had formed, her smile faded. "My mother will think I've gone stark raving mad."

He chuckled. "Surely it won't be that bad."

"You don't know my mother. She'll be offering us her congratulations and her condolences in a single breath."

How could he have forgotten about Lily's quaint, but kooky, family? The one who believed they were black widows? "My mother, the queen of eternal optimism. Your mother, Lucretia Borgia reincarnated. We've got to get these ladies together."

Eric felt an icy chill as Lily stepped out of the circle of his arms. She glared at him. "That's an awful idea."

Her abandonment put him in a contrary mood. "Why? Because you're having second thoughts?"

"Second, third and then some."

He set his jaw in a stubborn line. "You have to marry me, Lily. You don't have a choice."

She narrowed her eyes. "Oh? Why is that?"

"Because if you don't, I'll sue you for breach of promise."

She placed both hands on her hips in a defiant gesture, but she eyed him warily. "You wouldn't dare."

She was right. He wouldn't. But he'd fought too hard to get her to accept his proposal. He wasn't going to let her change her mind now.

"Look, Lily. Why don't we wait until after the wedding to tell our families? My mother lives in Tucson. Yours lives in Sedona. We'll get married on Saturday, then take a honeymoon trip touring Arizona, breaking the news to our respective families. They can't be too upset once the deed's already been done."

"I don't know, Eric."

He caught the slight hesitancy in her voice and moved in for the kill, assuming his most persuasive tone. "Come on, Lily. What do you say? It'll be fun."

"'Fun' isn't quite the word I'd use to describe it."

"But you'll do it?"

"Yes, I'll do it."

He released a slow breath of relief.

"I'm wise to you, Eric." She wagged a finger at him as though he were a naughty boy. "Don't think you can always sweet-talk me into doing things your way."

Eric shot her a devilish look. "So, you plan to resist each and every one of my whims?"

"Uh-huh."

"Too bad." He took a step toward her. "Because it's too late to go to work."

"Much too late," she agreed, sounding slightly out of breath.

"I was going to suggest we play hooky for the rest of the afternoon... to discuss our wedding plans. But I wouldn't want to be accused of bullying you into something you don't want to do." He snaked an arm around her waist and pulled her toward him, taking her lips in a gentle kiss.

The kiss deepened. Their bodies melded. He relished the feel of Lily's soft curves pressed against his hardness. The desire to be one with her, body and soul, overwhelmed him. Then he remembered his promise to wait for their wedding night.

Gathering his waning strength, Eric broke the kiss. He rested his chin on the top of her head, breathing in the scent of wildflowers. "On second thought, going to work may be the best choice after all. Staying here with you may be tempting fate."

Lily chuckled, a deep throaty sound. He felt the rise and fall of her breasts against his chest as she breathed a contented sigh.

He understood her contentment. The tension that had held them these past two months had eased. They were going to marry. Never before had he felt such a sense of fulfillment. He made a mental picture of this moment, framing it in his mind so that he'd never forget.

For the first time in his life, he finally understood why his clients made fools of themselves in the name of love, hoping against hope that the magic would last forever.

Lily was the kind of woman he could make a fool of himself over. She could almost make him believe in the fairy tale. She'd already made him wonder if there was such a thing as happily ever after.

Chapter Ten

"Mr. Fontaine, for the record, please state your full name and occupation."

Peter Fontaine, a thin, dark-haired man in his early forties, scowled at Eric from across the conference table. "You already know it."

"Yes. This is merely a formality," Eric explained, careful to hide his impatience. Rule number one in the practice of law—never allow the opposition to see you agitated. Anger and hostility only gave them fuel with which to fight.

But scratch the surface of his cool demeanor and you'd find a man who couldn't wait for this deposition to end. *Fontaine v. Fontaine* was his last case to wrap up before he married Lily. Tomorrow was his wedding day. Eric glanced at the angry man across the table. This was a hell of a way to welcome in his own attempt at marriage.

Fontaine released a harsh breath. "Peter Fontaine, illusionist."

Illusionist—a fancy term for a high-priced magician. Eric had caught Fontaine's show in Las Vegas last year. Aided by the glitz of pyrotechnical stunts, his act wasn't half bad. With his soon-to-be-ex-wife acting as his manager, Fontaine had built quite a reputation for himself in the nightclub circuit.

"Fontaine is your show name. For our records we need your legal birth name."

Fontaine removed a gold coin from the inside breast pocket of his baggy suit jacket. One-handed, he transferred the coin to the back of his hand and walked it from one knuckle to another. Eric had a feeling the trick, appearing merely to be a nervous habit, had a specific purpose. That is, to draw attention away from what was really happening in the deposition. Eric's gaze rested on the man's long, tapering fingers; he half expected the coin to disappear before his eyes.

"Mr. Fontaine," Eric said again. "Your birth name."

"Herbie Coggins," Fontaine said, his face puckered with distaste. "But I prefer my stage name, Fontaine."

Thin narrow face, long nose, beady eyes, he reminded Eric of a weasel. Eric carefully suppressed his feelings, not allowing the man to see his dislike. "Mr. Fontaine, I have your sworn statement revealing all your assets, liabilities and income. Do you acknowledge this statement as being a true representation of your net worth?"

The coin disappeared. "Yeah, sure."

"Mr. Fontaine, do you know a Mrs.—" Eric shuffled through a stack of papers. He knew the name. The search was a tension builder, an effect. He bit back a smile. Fontaine wasn't the only illusionist in the room. He picked up a sheet of paper. "A Mrs. Alice Thompson?"

Fontaine shrugged. "The name sounds familiar."

"Mrs. Thompson is very familiar with you, Mr. Fontaine."

Fontaine shifted in his chair.

In her seat next to Eric, Mrs. Fontaine muttered, "You slimy, son of a—"

Eric continued, "Or more correctly, Mrs. Thompson knows you as Herbie Coggins."

Fontaine shrugged again. "Yeah, I guess."

"Mrs. Thompson is a real-estate agent?"

"Yeah."

Eric picked up the stack of papers. "Mrs. Thompson has provided us with documents representing real estate transactions that she has handled for you during your marriage to my client. Real estate transactions that you've failed to mention in your sworn statement."

Fontaine gave him a cold stare. His lawyer picked up the documents and riffled through them.

Eric sat back in his chair and watched as Fontaine and his lawyer conducted a heated debate in hushed whispers. After months of negotiating with this greedy con man and with the help of the firm's private detective, they'd struck pay dirt. Fontaine had been caught redhanded in a lie. Eric allowed himself a moment of triumph. His client could finally expect a fair settlement.

Eric's thoughts drifted to Lily. He swore to himself their marriage would never end like this—facing each other across the divorce table. Lying, cheating, bickering. Eric's chest tightened. He would never hurt Lily that way. And he couldn't imagine Lily intentionally hurting him. Their marriage would be different. Theirs would be the one in three that lasted.

Theirs would be the one in three that lasted.

The force of those words struck him, taking his breath away. Their significance filled him with wonder. Two months ago he wouldn't have considered marriage as a possibility, let alone looked forward to it with such anticipation and optimism. Eric almost smiled. A lot of changes had occurred in two months' time.

Looking harried, Fontaine's lawyer said, "In light of this new evidence, I'd like to call a recess in the deposition. Mr. Fontaine and I need time to discuss how to proceed."

Fontaine stood, pointing a finger at Eric. "I don't care what new evidence you have—you aren't squeezing me for more of my money."

Mrs. Fontaine jumped to her feet. "Your money? If it wasn't for me, you wouldn't have any money. I'm the one who hustled to get you those nightclub dates. I'm the one who kept you sober so you wouldn't blow your reputation. If it wasn't for me, *Herbie,* you'd still be doing card tricks at birthday parties."

Fontaine's face flushed red with anger. He swung his gaze to Eric. "You really think you've got your hooks in me, don't you? You think I'll agree to anything you want."

Eric rose to his feet. "Mr. Fontaine, I suggest you calm down."

"Always the perfect answer, Mr. Attorney. You're ripping my life apart. Can't you show any emotion? Not even a hint of self-satisfaction for a job well done?" His beady eyes bulged in their sockets. "What are you, made of ice?"

Eric took a deep breath. "Mr. Fontaine—"

In a flicker of movement, Fontaine reached into his suit jacket, withdrew a small black pistol and pointed it directly at Eric's zipper. Eric's heart lurched, then thudded against his chest.

Fontaine snickered. "Don't look so cool now, do you, Mr. Attorney?"

"Herbie—you idiot—put that gun away," Mrs. Fontaine ordered.

"Mrs. Fontaine, let me handle this. I don't think it's a good idea to provoke him," Eric muttered.

"Yeah. Let your attorney handle it, Myra." He waved the gun. "Let's see what Mr. Cool has to say for himself. You've got to the count of five to give me a good reason not to shoot you, Mr. Attorney. One..."

Eric's mouth went dry.

"Two..."

His mind's eye conjured up a picture of Lily. Lily's beautiful face. Green eyes that sparkled like emeralds. The dimples dancing in her cheeks as she explained the mystery behind her family curse.

Eric tried to squeeze the memory from his mind. Lily's curse was the last thing he needed to think about. But for the briefest second, he questioned his doubt in magic and curses. For the first time, he wondered if he really was destined to meet with an early demise thanks to his pending marriage to Lily.

"Three..."

No. He refused to believe Lily had anything to do with this crazed man with a gun in his hand. Divorces were filled with passion, involving two people in highly emotional states. As an attorney he handled potentially volatile situations every day. There was no connection between marrying Lily and Fontaine's threat.

"Four, five. Time's up, Mr. Attorney."

Out of the corner of his eye, Eric saw Fontaine's lawyer, Mrs. Fontaine and the court stenographer hit the floor. Eric followed suit, diving for protection under the table. His reaction time proved a hair too late.

Eric heard a pop, then another, as a burning pain stung his backside.

"Lily, I think you'd better listen to this," her assistant said rushing into her office, shoving a portable radio into Lily's hands.

Lily smiled. "Ann, if this is another one of your rap songs—"

"Lily, I think it's about Eric."

"Eric?" Lily's heart skipped a beat. She popped on the radio's headphones and listened carefully to the tinny voice of the news announcer:

"Recapping the news bulletin, a shooting at the law offices of Franklin and Hirsch. One man injured, believed to be a divorce attorney representing Franklin and Hirsch. One man arrested. Details at the top of the hour."

Could it be Eric? A hot spill of panic raced through her veins. Not again, she told herself. This couldn't be happening again.

She threw down the radio and reached for the telephone to dial Eric's office. The phone rang before she had a chance to pick up the receiver. A cold chill of foreboding swept her body, quickly replacing the heat of panic, as she recognized Eric's secretary's voice.

"Where is he?" Lily asked simply.

"Maricopa General," Mrs. Hunter said. "But, Lily—"

"I'm on my way." Lily slammed the phone onto its cradle and grabbed her purse.

"Lily, you're too upset to drive. Let me take you." Ann placed a hand on her arm, stopping her headlong rush for the door.

Lily felt numb. "Thanks, but I need you to stay here at the bakery."

Reluctantly, Ann released her. "Promise me you'll call as soon as you hear anything . . . anything at all."

Lily nodded, then left.

The entrance to the hospital was crowded. Like scavengers searching for a morsel of food, reporters and camera men were scoping the halls, looking for a story. Lily shot them a distasteful glance, remembering the unwanted attention she'd received from reporters following the plane crash that had taken David's life. The memory felt like an omen. She pushed it from her mind.

"Lily."

Lily spun around, searching for the woman who'd called her name. Through the crowd, she spotted Mrs. Hunter, Eric's secretary.

"Look at you. You're as pale as a ghost," Mrs. Hunter said with a tsk. "I tried to tell you on the phone, but you wouldn't let me finish, so I came here. Eric's fine."

Lily said nothing. She'd broken every speed limit getting there. But still, the past twenty minutes had seemed to drag by, giving her too much time to think. By the time she'd pulled into the hospital parking lot, she'd convinced herself the worst had happened. That she had lost Eric. Now no amount of reassurance could soothe her. She had to see him for herself.

"You don't believe me, do you?" Mrs. Hunter sighed. "Come on, then. Let's go find Eric."

Mrs. Hunter pushed her way through the crowded lobby with Lily in tow. She marched up to the nurses' desk outside the emergency room. "We need to see a patient," she demanded.

The nurse, a tall, thin woman with sparrowlike features, opened the patient registry. "The patient's name?"

"Eric Mitchell."

The nurse snapped the registry closed. "Sorry, ma'am. You'll just have to wait outside along with everyone else."

Mrs. Hunter straightened her shoulders and shot the nurse a determined look. "I don't think you understand. I have to see him now."

The nurse planted her hands on her bony hips. "I don't think *you* understand. No one's getting through to see Mr. Mitchell unless they're a relative."

Mrs. Hunter jutted out her chin. "I'm his mother."

Lily's eyes widened in surprise.

Before she could object, Mrs. Hunter grabbed Lily's arm and hauled her up to the desk. "And this is his pregnant wife."

Lily strangled a moan.

The nurse reopened the registry and ran a finger over the file. "Mr. Mitchell didn't mention he was married."

"He didn't?" Lily asked, deciding to follow Mrs. Hunter's lead. She blinked hard, trying to appear shocked. "How could he have forgotten?"

Mrs. Hunter leaned confidingly toward the nurse. "Newlyweds," she whispered. "Look, he's just been shot. Do you expect him to remember everything?"

The nurse glanced from one to the other. Lily could almost hear her mind working, sizing them up, wondering what the chances were that two reporters would go this far for a story.

"I give up," she said, releasing a long-suffering sigh. "Follow me."

Saying a quiet prayer of thanks for Mrs. Hunter, Lily followed the nurse and Eric's secretary into the examining room. She stopped dead in her tracks. Overwhelming relief flooded her body as she spotted Eric sitting on the examining table. One sleeve of his shirt seemed to have been cut and the seam ripped. The ragged ends revealed a bandage wrapped around his forearm. The impatient scowl on his face softened as their eyes met.

"Your wife and mother are here, Mr. Mitchell," the nurse informed him.

Eric frowned, looking confused.

Lily stepped up to the table, carefully embracing him. "Thank goodness, you're okay."

"Mother?" he whispered, his breath warm against her ear.

"I'll explain later," Lily murmured, her lips lingering against his cheek. His face felt rough with the beginnings of a late-day beard. She closed her eyes and inhaled deeply, breathing in the familiar scent of citrus and spice. She wanted to shout her relief. Eric was alive.

"I told her you were okay," Mrs. Hunter interrupted. "She wouldn't believe me."

Eric grinned. "At least you tried . . . Mom."

"Mom, indeed," Mrs. Hunter harrumphed loudly, struggling to hide a pleased smile. She turned to Lily. "If you need me, I'll be outside."

Lily watched as Mrs. Hunter strode away, arm in arm with the skeptical nurse. Once they were alone, Lily turned on Eric. "What happened?"

Eric held out his bandaged arm. "I got a cut. Ten stitches. Can you believe it? This doctor acted as though it were no big deal when he put a needle and thread through my arm."

Lily persisted. "The radio said there was a shooting."

Eric muttered an oath. "Lily, it was nothing. Believe me. We were in the middle of a deposition, when my client's husband got a little upset. He pulled an air pistol out of his suit jacket just to scare me."

Lily touched the bandage with the tips of her fingers. "Obviously he did more than scare you."

Color crept across Eric's face. "The jerk had a BB gun. He shot off a couple of pellets. They hit me on my backside but bounced off without doing any harm." He grinned sheepishly. "I cut my arm on the table's metal leg when I ducked under it for protection."

The trembling chill returned. The thought of a man pointing a gun at Eric stunned her. Her worst fear blossomed, stretching cold petals of horror throughout her body. She wanted to hold Eric in her arms and protect him. But she had the awful feeling it was in her arms that Eric was most vulnerable.

A man in a white coat breezed into the emergency room, drawing her out of her disturbing reverie. He nodded a greeting.

"I'm Dr. Kirby. You must be Mrs. Mitchell."

Lily's heart thudded. She wondered why such an innocent statement could suddenly take on such a deadly connotation.

"How are we doing, Mr. Mitchell?" the doctor asked, looking at Eric's arm.

"*We* are ready to leave," Eric muttered.

The doctor smiled. "Not until you have your shot."

Lily gazed at the doctor, a question in her eyes. "Shot?"

"Mr. Mitchell cut himself on a metal object. He needs a tetanus shot," the doctor said, his tone brisk. As he spoke, the nurse appeared, carrying a tray with a cotton ball and syringe.

"I'm sure this isn't necessary," Eric said, ready to argue. "I had all my shots when I was a kid."

"Tetanus shots need to be updated," the doctor said, his tone allowing no arguments.

Eric scowled. "You'd think jabbing me with a needle and thread would be bad enough. But no, now I need a shot. Doc, I sure hope your malpractice insurance is up-to-date."

The doctor ignored Eric's threats. He nodded toward Eric but directed his question to Lily. "Is he always this cranky?"

Lily smiled. "Worse."

The doctor chuckled as he swabbed Eric's upper arm with the alcohol-laced cotton ball. When he picked up the syringe, Eric blanched.

Lily placed a reassuring hand on Eric's shoulder and whispered in his ear the reward he'd get for being a good boy. Eric was smiling as the needle broke the skin.

Chapter Eleven

" "Table's turned. Attorney gets his in the end.' " Lily read the headline aloud.

Eric's step faltered as he entered the kitchen.

Dressed in a pair of faded blue jeans, shirtless and barefoot, he looked irresistible. Her eyes lingered on the wide expanse of male chest, the trim waist and slender hips. She felt a familiar flush of heat warm her body.

Yesterday evening, they'd slipped away from the hospital, avoiding the reporters camped out front by using the rear exit. She had brought him home and pampered him with attention. Worried about his well-being, she'd stayed the night in the guest bedroom in case he needed her.

This morning, Eric's pallor had taken on a healthier cast. The bandage on his arm stood out against his tan skin, bringing memories of the shooting racing through her mind. She remembered what she had almost lost and felt the cold hand of reality grip her heart. She bit her lip to stop the trembling.

A frown creased his brow as he stepped up to where she stood at the kitchen counter.

"For someone who made the front page, you don't act very happy," she said, forcing a smile as she handed him the paper.

Eric rubbed the sleep from his eyes and squinted at the headlines. "Three paragraphs detailing how Fontaine shot my backside with a pellet gun. This type of publicity I don't need." He picked up a second paper and pointed to another headline: "Attorney injured while escaping madman with a BB gun." He groaned. "I'll never live it down. From now on, I'll be the butt of all attorney jokes." He scowled. "No pun intended."

"Eric, you should be thankful Mr. Fontaine didn't have a real gun," Lily said sternly. "If he did, you'd still be in the hospital, not recuperating at home in your own bed."

He tossed the newspaper onto the counter. His gaze softened as his eyes rested on her lips. "Hmm…going to my bed. Now, that sounds like a good idea."

A single look from Eric melted away all her good intentions. Despite the battle brewing within her, her body responded to his loving attention. A delicious shiver ran the length of her spine. There was no denying she still wanted him.

His eyes worked their magic downward, taking in the gentle swell of her breasts. Her skin tingled under the brush of his gaze.

She bit back a moan. "Eric, you're an injured man."

He grinned. "You're right—I am. And I think we should test the more vital parts of my anatomy until we're sure no other damage was done. After all, Lily, today is our wedding day."

Lily didn't comment. She needed to keep a clear head. But his presence was overwhelming, muddying her mind with confusion. She turned from his gaze and busied herself with gathering the scattered newspaper. Before she could step away, Eric grabbed her wrist, sending the papers spilling onto the floor. Pulling her against him, he kissed her long and hard.

At first she stiffened in his arms. Being this close to him would only make what she needed to do that much harder. But the more she resisted, the more demanding his kiss became. Lily stopped fighting. She allowed herself a moment to enjoy the solid feel of his body pressed against hers. Her worries and fears dimmed in comparison with the consuming pleasure his lips were creating inside her.

After a moment they broke apart. Lily leaned against him for support, gulping in deep drafts of air. Feeling the reassuring warmth of his bare skin against the palm of her hand, she gave her racing heartbeat time to return to normal.

Eric buried his face in her hair. "You smell good."

She smiled. "I smell like you. I borrowed your shampoo while you were asleep."

She'd hated the thought of putting on yesterday's clothes. Short of going home and changing, taking a shower had helped to make her feel refreshed.

"Sit down," she said, gathering the strength to push him away. "I'll make your breakfast."

"Breakfast?" He raised a brow. "I don't think I have anything in the house to eat. Unless you're heating up last night's pizza."

"Pizza for breakfast? Yuck," she said, grimacing. She poured a cup of coffee and handed it to him. "While you were asleep, I went shopping. I picked up a few things for you at the grocery store."

She strode to the refrigerator and took out the eggs and milk. Before she could close the door, Eric was behind her, glancing over her shoulder.

He opened the door wide. "Bacon, eggs, juice, butter." He gave her a puzzled look. "A few things? There's enough food here to feed an army."

She shrugged. "I just wanted to make sure you were well fed."

"Well fed?" He grinned. "Lily, we're getting married today. Food's the last thing I have on my mind."

Lily stepped past him, unable to say a word.

He grabbed her shoulder and whirled her around. She almost dropped the milk and eggs on the floor. She grasped them tight in her hands, using them as a buffer against the sudden glint of anger she saw in his eyes.

"We are getting married, aren't we?" he demanded.

She stared at him mutely. She'd hoped to delay this conversation for as long as possible. She told herself it was because she didn't want to upset Eric when he wasn't feeling well. But it was more than that. Nervously she licked her lips, tasting his kiss. She knew Eric wouldn't take her decision lightly. He would be angry. She wasn't sure if her resolve was strong enough to face a confrontation.

"Tell me you haven't changed your mind," he said, his voice quiet.

"No, not exactly."

"Not exactly?"

She took a deep breath. "Eric, I think we should postpone the wedding."

"Just until I'm feeling better, right?" he asked, his gaze wary.

"I'm not sure," she said hesitantly.

He slammed his fist on the counter. "I knew it. That's why you bought a truckload of groceries. Why you've been acting skittish when I come near you."

She tried to soothe his rising temper. "Now, Eric—"

"Whenever you start a sentence with 'Now, Eric' I know I'm in trouble."

She felt her resolve slipping. "Maybe we should discuss this when you're feeling better. When you're feeling a bit calmer."

"Uh-uh. Now." He gave his head a brisk shake. "This has to do with my getting shot at, doesn't it?"

"Of course it does." She sighed. "Eric, I nearly died when I found out some nut threatened you with a gun."

"A harmless BB gun," he reminded her.

"But it just as easily could have been a real gun." She shuddered, recalling the horror she had felt when she'd learned of the shooting.

"Lily, I won't let you blame yourself for this."

"How can I not? I finally agree to marry you, and you get shot at. That's too much of a coincidence even for you to explain away."

He cupped her chin, forcing her to look directly into his eyes. "What happened yesterday could have happened at any time. Marriages are based on passion. Emotions run hot during a divorce. Sometimes they explode. Being a divorce attorney is a hazardous job. That's a fact, Lily. It has nothing to do with you or your curse."

"I don't believe it," she said simply. "David's trip wasn't supposed to end in a crash, either. But it did, and I lost him. I'm not going to count the days waiting until I lose you, too."

A tiny vein pulsed violently on the side of his neck. "How long a postponement are we talking about? A week? A month?"

"Until after the baby is born. Then if you still want to marry me—"

"No way," he shouted.

Lily jumped, gripping the milk and eggs tight against her breasts. She'd never seen him so angry. "Eric, listen to me. This doesn't mean we can't see each other. I just think it would be better if we let things cool down a bit. Go back to the way it used to be."

"You mean, when I was just a friend?" he asked with a bitter twist to his lips.

She shrugged helplessly. "I don't know—I guess."

"Or maybe you want a bit more," he said, his expression harsh. "Maybe when the mood strikes, I could be an occasional roll in the hay. That should ease your lonely widow's needs."

She breathed in sharply. He was being deliberately crude. She'd hurt him, and now he was lashing back at her.

"When are you going to stop hiding behind that curse of yours, Lily?" He shot her an impatient look. "Are you ever going to tire of playing the grieving widow?"

She swallowed hard at the lump of emotion in her throat.

He raked a hand through his hair, looking frustrated and angry. "And after the baby is born? What guarantee do I have that you won't change your mind and decide *not* to marry me after all? Do you expect me to play Uncle Eric to my own child?"

Tears stung her eyes. She wanted to give in, to cry for the pain they were causing each other. "I wouldn't do that to you."

"That's right. Because I won't let you. I'll take you to court, Lily. I'll file for custody if I have to."

"You can't," she gasped.

He narrowed a gaze at her. "Watch me."

A weight pressed against her chest, making it difficult for her to breathe. "You signed a contract. The donor release form."

"I'm a lawyer, Lily. Breaking contracts is what I do."

She fought the rising tide of panic. "You wouldn't do that do me."

He looked at her, one brow raised in question.

"You wouldn't hurt me that way." She swallowed hard. "You're my friend, Eric."

He stared at her for a long moment, unspeaking. Then, with a shake of his head, he laughed. There was no amusement in his tone. "It all comes down to being friends, doesn't it, Lily? We became friends because of David. As a *friend,* you asked me to be a sperm donor. Now you're asking me to give up my child because we're *friends.*"

"I'm sorry," she said. Her voice sounded weak, the words hopelessly inadequate.

"I'm sorry, too." He averted his eyes, staring at the tiled floor beneath his feet. "You're right. Taking you to court would be cruel. I can't hurt you that way." He lifted his gaze. His expression was devoid of emotion. But his eyes were filled with pain. "Being your friend just isn't enough. If you won't marry me, then I can't see you. It hurts *me* too much."

She took a step toward him, then stopped. "Eric, I didn't plan for any of this to happen."

"I didn't plan to fall in love with you, either."

The words echoed in the quiet room.

He loved her.

Lily felt her heart go out to him. She wanted to comfort him and tell him that his love was returned. But she knew it would only cause him more pain, because she couldn't carry out the promise of love. She didn't have the courage to marry him. She'd rather deal with a broken heart than take a chance and lose him forever.

"Lily."

She looked at him questioningly.

"We're in my house," he reminded her, his voice hoarse with emotion. "You're the one who has to leave."

She nodded, feeling numb inside as she hurried from the kitchen. She made it to the front door before she realized she still held the eggs and milk in her hands.

Eric hadn't moved from the kitchen counter; his expression was unchanged.

Without a word, she returned the food to the refrigerator, then turned on her heel to escape.

"Lily."

His voice stopped her.

"If you change your mind..." The words trailed off. He released a harsh breath, then said nothing.

Lily heard the frustration in his voice. She felt his pain. In Eric's arms, she'd thought their love was invincible. She dared to hope for a life with him. She should have known she was destined to spend her life alone. At least she'd always have her memories. And his child.

With all the strength she could muster, she forced herself to leave.

Chapter Twelve

Lily stepped back, gripping the pastry bag in her hand and surveyed her handiwork. In silver icing on the top of an anniversary cake due to be sent out that afternoon she'd scrolled the words *Happy Twenty-fifth, Lily and Eric.* She groaned with frustration. It was the second time in a row she'd made the same mistake.

She couldn't shake thoughts of Eric.

Guilt was ruining her life.

She plopped down onto a stool and allowed herself a moment to wallow in self-pity. In the two weeks since she'd last seen Eric, her life had gone from bad to worse. Monsoon winds had settled over Phoenix, kicking up unexpected storms and oppressive weather. The days were suffocating. The nights were lonely and restless.

Despite the fact her appetite had taken a nose dive, she'd been gaining weight at a steady pace. This morning she'd discovered she couldn't close the zipper of her favorite jeans. She now had large and unappealing to add to her faults, though guilt still made it to the top of the list.

Guilt for the pain she'd caused Eric.

Tears burned her eyes. She tried to push the memory of the last time they were together from her mind.

Her only consolation was keeping busy at the bakery. Now it seemed she couldn't concentrate on her work. She glared at the cake. Proof of this was staring her in the eye.

She might as well admit the truth. She missed Eric terribly. Not a minute went by that she didn't think about him. Their last encounter was as fresh in her mind as though it had happened yesterday. She drew in a shaky breath. She could still see the pain reflected in his brown eyes. Pain she'd caused by refusing to marry him.

She felt her mood slip another notch as she fell under the heavy weight of self-flagellation. Lily grimaced. She was going beyond wallowing in self-pity.

The metal legs of the stool rasped against the tiled floor as she scooted to her feet. She picked up a spatula and scraped *Lily and Eric* off the cake. The defiant gesture didn't make her feel any better. Her chest tightened. The cake blurred as tears filled her eyes.

She blinked away the tears and tried to pull herself out of her miserable mood. She wasn't the only one to blame for her misery. Eric was the one who had insisted they couldn't see each other. Two weeks had passed without a word from him. Didn't he care about her? About their baby?

Of course he cared about her and the baby. Eric could have taken her to court. He could have forced her to recognize his rights as a parent. But he hadn't done that. He knew the pain a custody battle would cause. He loved her too much to hurt her. He'd proved beyond a doubt that his love was unselfish.

Lily found herself teetering on the brink of another bout of tears. Being angry felt better, she reminded herself. Why did Eric have to insist on marriage? If he wasn't so stubborn, they'd still be together, not at opposite ends of Phoenix. Her anger simmered. If she didn't love him so much, she'd almost say he deserved to marry her. Losing him to the curse couldn't be any worse than the pain he was putting her through right now.

Losing him?

She caught her breath. The realization hit hard. She was mourning Eric as though she'd already lost him. As though he were already dead.

Eric was right. She'd gotten so good at being a widow, she didn't know how to be anything else.

Lily sat down hard on the stool, filled with a new, almost painful awareness. There were no guarantees that they'd spend the rest of their lives together. Instead of acting like the grieving widow, she should be treasuring the moments they did have. She should be with him, grabbing at her chance for happiness with both hands, not blubbering over something that might or might not happen.

She swallowed hard at the stubborn lump of guilt in her throat. She had a lot to feel guilty about. She'd overreacted to Eric's brush with a gunman. She'd used it as an excuse to back out of their engagement because she didn't want to admit the truth.

She loved him so much she was scared. And she was allowing that fear to control her life, her happiness.

The admission left her feeling oddly relieved, as though a burden had been lifted from her shoulders. A love as strong as theirs didn't happen overnight. She'd fallen in love with Eric long before she'd asked him to be a sperm donor. By asking him, she'd merely taken her first step in admitting her love.

She sniffed loudly, brushing away a tear. As usual, her realizations were too little, too late. She wouldn't blame Eric if he'd given up on her. After all, she'd already broken more promises to him than she cared to remember. She'd promised not to let her pregnancy come between their friendship, but it did. She promised to marry him, but she changed her mind.

Lily slapped the spatula on the counter. She'd had enough self-pity. Somehow she had to convince Eric this time she truly believed they had a chance at forever.

Listlessly Eric picked up a file off his desk and began to read. A new case, *Richards v. Richards*. This one involved kids. Two boys—Joey, age four; Bobby, age six. His heart skipped a beat. He forced himself to read on. Reason for initiating divorce procedure: irreconcilable differences. He wondered if Joey and Bobby thought the differences in their parents' marriage were irreconcilable.

Eric slammed the file back down onto his desk. What was wrong with him? In the highly charged atmosphere surrounding a divorce, an attorney had to stay detached from his clients' problems. Staying neutral was the only way he could serve their best interests.

Since he'd allowed Lily to walk out of his life, he'd lost his edge. He couldn't separate himself from his clients' emotions. Damn, if he kept this up, he'd end up losing half his cases.

He glanced at the phone and felt the urge to pick it up. He gave a growl of frustration. How much longer could he hold out? He couldn't count the number of times he'd started to call Lily, just to slam the receiver down, cursing himself for being a fool.

He sighed. No, he was worse than a fool. A fool would have given up by now. Lily's message had been loud and clear. She didn't need him in her life.

He'd been wrong.

She didn't love him. If she did, they would be married by now.

He stood, crossing the office to the bank of windows overlooking downtown Phoenix. The truth was, being married didn't seem as important as it had two weeks ago. He loved her so much that if Lily walked through that door right now he'd take her any way he could get her, marriage or no marriage.

Music filtered in through the closed door of his office, drawing him out of his brooding thoughts. Eric frowned. Brass horns? Guitars? The music grew louder.

Eric crossed to his desk and picked up the phone. As he buzzed his secretary, a knock sounded at his door.

Mrs. Hunter poked her head around the door, a smile stretching across her face. "I think you'd better come out here, boss."

Eric scowled. "What the—?"

"No arguments," Mrs. Hunter chided. "Just come on."

She disappeared.

Eric released a harsh breath and followed.

In the outer office a small crowd had gathered. In the center of the crowd stood a *mariachi band*. Eric recognized Mr. Ramirez immediately. He'd hired Ramirez's band to play for Lily. Eric felt a niggling of hope rise in his chest. He glanced around the office, looking for her familiar face.

"Hello, Mr. Mitchell," Ramirez said, approaching Eric with a broad smile. "We've been asked to play for you today. Our first song is about a young man whose heart has been broken. In this song his lover asks for forgiveness.'' With a flick of his hand, he motioned for the band to start.

Loud, beautiful music filled the tiny office. Eric felt the floor vibrating beneath his feet. The paintings on the walls wobbled from their perches. Mrs. Hunter's phone danced on her desk.

His fellow office workers were smiling, amused by the spectacle.

Eric scowled. There was still no sign of Lily. For all he knew, Mrs. Hunter could have ordered the group. She'd been trying to coax him out of his dark mood for the past two weeks. He discarded that idea as quickly as it had risen. No, not Mrs. Hunter. She knew this band would stir up memories of Lily. She wouldn't be that cruel.

It had to be Lily. No one else would embarrass him this way. His impatience grew with each beat of the music.

Finally the song ended.

"Thank you, Mr. Ramirez," Eric began. "Now, who—"

"Our next song is about star-crossed lovers."

The music began again, drowning out Eric's moan of frustration.

Then he spotted a familiar face. His heart pounded in his chest, competing with the pulsing beat of the brass horns filling his office. Lily was pushing her way through the crowd.

Soon she stood before him, looking flushed and uncertain. She ran a nervous hand through her auburn curls.

Eric waited.

She took a deep breath. "I have a proposition for you, counselor."

A slow grin lifted one corner of his mouth. "What sort of proposition?"

"Don't worry, it's definitely *not* business," she said. Her expression was sober, but her eyes glittered.

He crossed his arms over his chest to stop himself from pulling her into a sweeping embrace. "This I have to hear."

"It's like this. I'm looking for a husband."

Eric's grin widened.

Lily continued, the words spilling out in a rush. "Not just any man will fit the bill, mind you. He must have a persistent nature."

"You mean stubborn?"

"Uh-huh." Lily nodded. "He must be ready to take on the challenges life may throw his way."

"Like curses and bad luck."

Lily smiled. "Exactly."

He tried to appear uncertain. "Sounds like a pretty tough job. What sort of benefits could your husband expect?"

"A lifetime of love and happiness."

He raised a brow. "A lifetime?"

"I can't promise forever, but how does the next forty or fifty years sound to you?"

Relief flooded his body. "Not bad, not bad at all."

Lily snapped her fingers. "Oh, did I mention there's an extra bonus to sweeten the pot? A baby who needs her father."

"Her, eh? Still think it's a girl?"

"Girls run in my family." Lily smiled. "Some things just can't be changed. So what do you say, counselor? Are you ready to accept my proposal?"

"And if I'm not?"

She waved a hand at the mariachi band. "Mr. Ramirez will just keep playing until you change your mind."

He chuckled. "In that case, you've got yourself a deal."

Eric pulled her into his arms and kissed her soundly.

A cheer went up throughout the room. The music swelled.

Breathless, they broke apart.

"I love you, Eric," she shouted.

His heart soared. The words sounded like heaven. He knew how hard they had been for her to say. "I love you, too, Lily," he said, pressing his lips to her ear so she could hear him over the noise. "I have a confession to make. In another two minutes, I would have been out this door, looking for you. I'd already decided I wasn't going to let another day go by without you in my life."

Her eyes shimmered with emotion.

"I'm not taking any more chances. Lily, I know this judge who'd be more than willing to perform a wedding ceremony any time—any day."

Her radiant smile melted the last of his doubts.

"What are we waiting for, counselor? Let's get married. Now."

Epilogue

"Whew." Lily collapsed against the comfort of the leather bucket seat. Slowly she unclenched the death grip she had on the door handle. "That was a bad one."

Eric glanced at his watch, then shot her a concerned look. "Are you okay?"

"I'm fine. Watch the road."

He released an exasperated breath. "Lily, would you relax? It's two o'clock in the morning. The streets are practically deserted. I'm only going twenty in a forty-mile-an-hour zone. Nothing's going to happen."

Another spasm of pain gripped her stomach. "Ahhhh..."

Eric checked his watch. "Two minutes. They're only two minutes apart. What does that mean?"

"It means," she said, her teeth clenched, "if you don't step on it, Eric, we're going to have this baby in the front seat of your Porsche."

He needed no further encouragement. Eric tromped on the accelerator. Tires squealing, the speedometer jumped to fifty. The momentum pressed Lily farther into her seat.

"Eric—" She clutched the door handle again. This time in fear.

He patted her knee. "Hold on, Lily. With our history of bad luck, I'm not taking any chances. You are not—I repeat—not delivering this baby in the front seat of my car."

The pain crested, taking her breath away. She stopped arguing.

Soon Eric pulled into the hospital's emergency room entrance. Within minutes, she was whisked into the delivery room.

"Are you okay?" she asked her husband between the pains.

The delivery-room nurse gave her an incredulous stare. "Honey, you're the one having this baby. Not him."

Lily smiled sheepishly. "He has a weak stomach."

The nurse shot him a skeptical glance. "A fainter, eh?"

Eric, now dressed in hospital greens, lifted his chin defiantly. "I'll be fine. I've been through Lamaze classes. I've got a certificate to prove it."

The nurse snorted. "I've scraped plenty of men off the floor who've said the exact same thing."

"Look, I'm a lawyer and I've been shot at." He narrowed his eyes. "I can handle anything."

"Right," the nurse said. She scooted a stool toward Eric. "Start getting dizzy, sit down. Got it?"

"Got it," Eric grumbled.

Lily grinned.

Eric squeezed her hand. "You've got to stop worrying about me and concentrate on yourself and our daughter. We've made it this far. Nothing's going to stop us now."

"I hope you're right." She clutched his hand as another pain gripped her body. "I think this is it. I feel I have to push."

"Already?" Eric looked worried.

The doctor and staff of nurses took over. In a flurry of motion and a bout of seemingly endless pain, their child was born.

Exhausted, Lily collapsed back against the delivery table, giving herself a moment to replenish her energy. She smiled drowsily, the miracle of birth settling around her like a warm, comforting blanket.

"I'll be damned," Eric murmured at her side.

Her heart thudded as panic seized her. Lily struggled to rouse herself. "What's wrong? The baby? Is she okay?"

Eric laid a calming hand on her shoulder, his eyes dancing with amusement. "The baby's fine. Only she's a he."

"A boy? We had a boy?"

He chuckled. "Looks as though we're going to have to change those pink bunnies in the nursery to something a little more masculine."

"Eric," she said, her voice filled with wonderment.

Eric frowned, his expression concerned. "What is it?"

"You're still here."

"Of course I am, Lily." He looked offended. "Did you think I'd chicken out and leave."

She shook her head. "No. I mean, you lived to see our baby being born. The curse . . . it really has been broken."

He smiled. "So that's what all this concern's been about. Do you mean to tell me that after all this time, you still had your doubts?"

"Well . . ."

"Listen to me, Lily. As far as I'm concerned, that curse ended when I fell in love with you."

She considered this for a moment. "Eric, do you remember the day we talked about the curse?"

He nodded. "I remember. You thought love started the curse."

"Do you remember what you said? You said, maybe just being in love wasn't enough. That love had to be proved by doing something unselfish."

He frowned. "I did?"

"Don't blow your romantic image now, Eric." She chuckled. "You were right. You could have taken me to court and filed for custody when I wouldn't marry you. But you didn't, because you loved me too much to hurt me. Eric, that was the most unselfish thing anyone's ever done for me."

He sighed. "Can we forget about the curse now, Lily? I've got lots of plans for our future. Things I'd much rather be thinking about. Like picking out a boy's name. And having lots of brothers and sisters to keep our son company."

Lily moaned.

Eric pressed his lips to her forehead. "I love you, Lily. I always will."

"I know, Eric." She smiled, feeling content and happy. "I know."

* * * * *

Silhouette celebrates motherhood in May with...

Debbie Macomber
Jill Marie Landis
Gina Ferris Wilkins

in

Three Mothers & a Cradle

Join three award-winning authors in this beautiful collection you'll treasure forever. The same antique, hand-crafted cradle connects these three heartwarming romances, which celebrate the joys and excitement of motherhood. Makes the perfect gift for yourself or a loved one!

A special celebration of love,

Only from

Silhouette®

—where passion lives.

Take 4 bestselling love stories FREE

Plus get a FREE surprise gift!

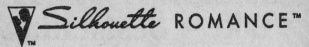

Silhouette ROMANCE™

is proud to present

The spirit of the West—and the magic of romance…Saddle up and get ready to fall in love Western-style with WRANGLERS AND LACE. Starting in May with:

Daddy Was a Cowboy
by Jodi O'Donnell

Jamie Dunn was determined to show Kell Hamilton she was the best ranch hand he'd ever hired. But what would her handsome boss do when he learned she had another full-time career—as a mother?

Wranglers and Lace: Hard to tame—impossible to resist—these cowboys meet their match.

SL-1

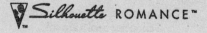

**Five unforgettable
couples say "I Do"...
with a little help
from their friends**

Always a Bridesmaid!

Always a bridesmaid, never a bride...that's
me, Katie Jones—a woman with more taffeta
bridesmaid dresses than dates! I'm just one of
the continuing characters you'll get to know in
ALWAYS A BRIDESMAID!—Silhouette's new
across-the-lines series about the lives, loves...and
weddings—of five couples here in Clover, South
Carolina. Share in all our celebrations! (With so
many events to attend, I'm sure to get my own
groom!)

In June, **Desire** hosts
THE ENGAGEMENT PARTY by Barbara Boswell

In July, **Romance** holds
THE BRIDAL SHOWER by Elizabeth August

In August, **Intimate Moments** gives
THE BACHELOR PARTY by Paula Detmer Riggs

In September, **Shadows** showcases
THE ABANDONED BRIDE by Jane Toombs

In October, **Special Edition** introduces
FINALLY A BRIDE by Sherryl Woods

Don't miss a single one—wherever
Silhouette books are sold.